The Carrionflower Had Claimed Its Prey . . .

Demsing had turned the tables on the assassin who had stalked him, but time was short, and he must learn what he could from his doomed pursuer.

Caught in the carnivorous plant's deadly grip, lulled by its hallucinogenic fragrance, still her lovely, blurred mouth worked, tried to shape words: ". . . can't stand it. Give me . . ."

Demsing drew his knife. "Who are you? Why follow me?"

Her body moved in the throes of some deep inner convulsion, then her eyes focused on him. "Can't die . . . you won . . . kill me . . ." And then, the answer that would buy her peace eternal: "Vollbrecht . . ."

Now the enemy had a name, but who or what was Vollbrecht?

M.A. FOSTER
has also written:

THE WARRIORS OF DAWN
THE GAMEPLAYERS OF ZAN
THE DAY OF THE KLESH
WAVES
THE MORPHODITE
TRANSFORMER
OWL TIME

PRESERVER

M.A. Foster

DAW BOOKS, INC

DONALD A. WOLLHEIM, PUBLISHER

1633 Broadway, New York, NY 10019

DAW Collectors Book No. 652

FOR MAURICE G. FOSTER, 1903–1970

First Printing, November 1985

1 2 3 4 5 6 7 8 9

PRINTED IN U.S.A.

1

> The only interesting part of a drama is the underlying skeleton of the morality play. The issue is not that the good guys versus the bad guys is shallow, banal and juvenile. That it undeniably is. But rather that, without the morality play, there simply is no way to distinguish good guy from bad guy. Whatsoever.
>
> —H.C., Atropine 1984

Demsing knew that he was being followed and had made careful allowances. His shadow was skilled and made remarkably few betrayals; of that he could be certain, having tested the situation to make sure. What remained to trouble him was that, even now, he could not determine the purpose of the surveillance, nor could he assign a probable originator to it. However, he knew this spoke of a degree of risk to himself he could not afford to misunderstand. He did not reason this out, but perceived it virtually immediately, instinctively; survivors of Teragon did no less and lived long.

Although it was night, the glow from the city meant no particular advantage. In fact, for some operations, so-called daylight was equally good or better: the white dwarf which was Teragon's primary was small in the sky, and Teragon's thin atmosphere did not scatter much light, so shadows were both sharp and deep.

He was working his way higher into one of the older areas which had been built up into a gently rounded hill, long overgrown and encrusted with minor holdings along the slopes. He used walks, wheelways, and foot-alleys when convenient, but he also took shortcuts across courts, atriums, walls, swung on exposed reclamation lines and cableways, and even some roofs. Around him as he worked his way, the city surrounded him as far as he could see. The entire landscape was city, but not a city of soaring towers and intimidating giant structures; rather an erratic, softly rounded, coral-like organic growth which would have soon smothered abrupt forms. The individual units were simple blocky shapes with the edges rounded off and most roofs domed. The material was invariably *kamen*, the universal recyclable residue of the planet's interior, its colors pale pastels or off-whites, streaked and stained with organic residues. Blocks piled haphazardly, stacked in groups, and forming little hillocks separated by gulfs, which were not accidents of topography but only places which hadn't yet been filled in. It looked like preserved photographs from old Earth depicting a type of city called a *Casbah*, and from the outside it was secretive and reassuring at the same time. Inside those structures was where the fear lay. About a third of the units were lit within, which gave a magic quality to the still landscape.

Demsing knew that from any point on the planet, the view was more or less the same. *Which saves us travel money*, he added to himself. The city covered the entire planet all the way to the poles, which, owing to Teragon's rapid rotation and severe tilt as well as the recycling of the planet's internal energy, were not especially different from other points.

He hoped that his shadow, skilled as it might be, could not yet draw conclusions about where he was leading it. He thought that his path had been suitably random, deliberately giving the impression, in accordance with the suspected skill level of the tracker, of a simple attempt to shake a pursuer. He did not worry about being anticipated and run to earth, because, strictly speaking, he had no earth to run to. *That, too, was the code of Teragon.*

Now he was nearing the top of one of the hills, half-trotting easily in a relaxed, ground-covering lope along a deserted alley-way which was used to demarcate the upper-class places, higher up the slope, from the proles below. At the point he was looking for, he scaled up a drain line onto the low privacy wall and began sprinting across wall-lines and roofs, carefully skirting walled little gardens where increasingly deadly traps awaited the unwary; some were mechanical, some electronic, and the deadliest were the living forms. And as he neared the top of Ararry Rise, the traps would become still more deadly. He counted on that.

Now he was almost at the summit, and as he passed along a low wall separating sectors, he caught a faint trace of a scent he had been waiting to find. It had a harsh aromatic pungency overlain with a sweetness so intense it was cloying: Carrionflower in predative phase, close enough to be dangerous and cleverly concealed, as was its habit. Demsing knew that whoever was behind him could also pick up this peculiar scent and understand its meaning. And so now the game became deadly.

As far as he knew, no one knew where Carrionflowers had originated, or precisely what they were. They combined attributes of plant, animal, and fungus with a sophisticated ease that spoke of a long evolution somewhere where things were radically different from the way humans usually found them. Essentially, a Carrionflower was a semimobile preying plantlike organism which preferred flesh for its main diet and actively sought it out. It captured by luring its prey within reach with psychosexual pheronomes and hallucinogens of enormous power, and then tapping into the captured organism with vinous, ropy tendrils. The victim would be stung, paralyzed, and kept alive by intravenous feeding of glucose while the plant replenished its store of required chemical compounds, and seeded offspring from a store of previously fertilized gametes. It was said that the plant provided its unwilling hosts with psychedelic hallucinations of unsurpassed detail and clarity. Sometimes distraught souls would seek one out, imagining that the plant would provide a vision of paradise while feeding on it. In fact, it created and amplified chemically whatever might be the leaning of the mood of the victim, and so for one deeply depressed, giving oneself to a Carrionflower was in truth an invitation to hell unplumbed.

Demsing breathed deeply, to take in as much of the scent as he could before subtle trace compounds concealed within its brew shut off his perception of his own sense of smell. For a moment, he felt nothing; then came a heightened sense of clarity, a lift, a confidence. But yet no images, nothing concrete. The concealed plant was, somewhere in its tissues, registering the presence of prey that was not yet close enough to identify so it could attune its chemistry. He knew this one; the Llai Tong kept one near their training halls, and this particular plant was old and wise and very sly.

Contact! Demsing's sense of smell vanished as if it had been switched off, and simultaneously he felt an unexpected, unexplained sexual desire in his loins—unfocussed and unpersonalized, but very sudden and very strong, like a panicky urge to defecate. He ignored it as much as he could, suppressed it, and continued carefully, extra-consciously, along the way he had previously chosen. He thought he knew where this plant usually kept its main body, and he wanted to come as close as he could.

And now he began to catch hints of flickering images, almost-memories of females he had known, evanescent shifting pictures that vanished as fast as they appeared. Nearer to the heart's desire, that was the word; Carrionflower found out what your resonance was by chemistry and tuned you up to the point of madness. Even as he made himself remember this, it also occurred to him out of nowhere that he had indeed come to this place at this time to meet Sherith, and so indeed was she here, waiting for him, melting, ardent, in this garden, all he had to do was step into it, she waited in the shadows for him.

The urge was intense and irresistible. But he knew and could not forget that the real Sherith was dead, and so while the powerful chemical illusion haunted him, his own mind generated images to match the chemistry. *Sherith is dead*, he repeated, opening himself and allowing the response to that death to grasp him, as he never allowed it to in ordinary life. It was enough; the hold of the Carrionflower was broken, and once again his present reality returned to focus. He continued over a low wall, up a short drainpipe, across a roof with a low dome bulging its center. He glanced back across the landscape of the starlit city, spreading to the horizon. A flashback caught him, entangling his mind momentarily with a nonsense verse he totally misconstrued: *Oh little town of Bethlehem*, followed by an image of a much smaller version of the same city, with groves of peculiar trees with feathery, drooping tops. But the sensation of desire slackened a little, leaving him shaken and weak with the effort of denial. *Yes, but that was a lifesaving denial!*

He still had no perception of a sense of smell, and was still getting images and flickers of memories or pseudomemories, but the effects were now noticeably weaker. He stopped in a patch of deep shadow, and concealed himself beside an exhalator vent from somewhere deeper inside, which helped dilute the chemical barrage which the damned plant was emitting.

But unexpectedly, suddenly, the surge of desire came again, rose alarmingly and Demsing began moving, haltingly, exerting all his will to hold himself back, and it was not enough! It was close! And it could move, if it had to, itself. He groped in one of the shallow pockets of his coverall for an ampule of Atropine, but before he could administer it, he hallucinated a powerful image: a young man or perhaps late-adolescent. Demsing, bemused, did not object to that per se, but what puzzled him was that the image was, however clear, of no one he had ever known, that he could remember. The image, however attractive, was of a stranger. But, tantalizingly, he could almost put a name to the boy. He experienced a momentary confusion, because some still-conscious part of his mind knew that this was one of the limitations of the system of perception which the Carrionflower exploited: the mind of the intended victim *always* keyed the attractant to an image in memory, specifically a memory of a real person, not a projection.

The boy was slim and intensely vital, with clear and well-defined features, and a most peculiar mustache, soft and close to the skin, trimmed out (or not growing) in the center of his lip, drooping lazily at the corners of his mouth. Demsing almost reached for it, but he also insisted, even as he reached with an impossible lust for that face, that he had never known such a person, and for an instant his mind divided into two warring parts, and that conflict broke the hold of the plant. It tried to compensate by making the image even sharper, but the details were becoming blurry and Demsing was able to shake it off. Soon, it faded out entirely, and was replaced by a nearly uncontrollable urge to run as fast as possible from this place, in any direction. The fear was palpable.

Demsing smiled to himself, knowing that the trap he had set had indeed worked. The plant had picked up another prey, shifted to it, locked on, and had accomplished a successful catch. It always put out a warn-off chemical. He put the remembered ampule of Atropine away, and reached for another ampule of somewhat more specific effects, which he used, grimacing at the sting of it where he drove the point in.

Presently his senses returned to him. He waited, unmoving, measuring out the time it would take the Carrionflower to complete its connections with its new host. But while he waited, the image which the plant had caused him to hallucinate came clearly back to him. That, too, was unusual. A boy, or young man, with an odd mustache, distinctive and memorable. In the background, he could sense somehow that a city was burning, and there was an oppressive sense of dread, of onrushing, slowly magnificent doom, which had only been lightened by the sensual encounter he had had with . . . him. The name still eluded him. Still the image did not match any conscious memory, and there was now something else he had not seen before: in the image, he was perceiving the unknown nameless young man from a woman's point of view. He was *her* lover, not his. Right. It had been difficult seeing this at first, but once one caught on, it was obvious. He shook his head, hard, as if to clear away the cobwebs of a too-vivid nightmare, and thought, cynically, *Nice kid, that one, yeah, but I've never been a woman. Too bad!*

Back in the present, he reflected that, after all, the trap had worked, and about now, it would be time to slip down there and see what had fallen into the Carrionflower's embrace. Perhaps that might tell him something. But without delay: the Llai Tong certainly possessed chemoreceptors in their compound which would now be telling some unsleeping guard that their pet had caught someone. They would be interested, too. Maybe more than he.

The garden of the Tong appeared to be the typical rooftop garden of this sort of level, appreciably larger than most, but not greatly different from other places this high up on the rise. The predominant vegetation was of the hardy stock which everyone presumed to be native: sturdy, twisted fibrous trunks and small, fleshy leaves. Many of these were sensitive and semi-mobile and followed the rapid path of Primary across the dark sky of the painfully short day of Teragon.

He dropped soundlessly down onto the patio floor and examined each part of the garden closely. After a careful search, he found it in a dark corner, more or less where he had expected it to be. The main body of the plant looked to be an ancient, short tree-trunk, sinuous and twisted as if it had been out in hostile climes for centuries. It appeared rigid, and wooden; neither was true. All parts of the organism were slowly mobile, and it seemed to capture its prey by simply anticipating it, as a human might capture much-swifter flies in its hand by anticipating where the fly *would be*, not where it was, or had been. Then all one had to do was *be there*. But it was easy to understand how a human could do that, with a brain thousands of times the size of the fly's entire body; more difficult to comprehend how a hundred-kilo thing which looked like a cross between a bristlecone pine and a strangler fig, and which seemed to have nothing in its structure resembling either brain or nerves, could anticipate a human, or indeed any animal. *There was always the last category: OTHER*, he thought. *No system ever maps the universe 100 percent. It is a deadly arrogance to imagine that one could.*

Speed itself was of no ultimate advantage to the anticipated fly: neither in some cases did the maneuvering of a human avail against the uncanny powers of the Carrionflower. This one had clasped its prey to itself near the base of the trunk by rootlike branches which looked as if they had grown that way. It was already attached, and so that was that. Nothing, or very little, one could do about it, once it was attached and feeding. At any event, nothing absolute you could do in haste. It would kill the victim and defend itself. Once in a great while, an inexperienced Carrionflower might be persuaded to release a catch, but the process required a surrogate catch, and an excessively long time. They *were* treelike in their patience. At this moment, Demsing had little time, no prey, and very little patience. He stepped closer to examine the catch, repressing a crawling sensation of horror which was not completely caused by emanations from the plant.

This one had been a girl. Branches clasped her limbs and body in a parody of an embrace, and vinous tendrils touched her at several places he could see. Her clothing was disarrayed, but not removed: the plant never removed clothing, but simply grew through it. Her face was distorted, her head thrown back, and her mouth was opened in a grimace of mingled ecstasy and horror. While he watched, he could see her breathing shallowly and rapidly, and he could also see her abdomen contracting as if in the throes of the sexual act. A pale trumpetlike flower hovered directly above her uplifted face, a tiny bladder in its base working insistently, like a pulse, drenching her nervous system in hallucinogens which it synthesized on the spot, tuned by chemical feedback to the exact requirements of control of her body.

Demsing saw enough to identify the girl as a *Kobith* of the Wa'an* School of Assassins, an organization of impressive and admirable techniques, composed primarily but not exclusively of women. This girl was the nearest available example, in this universe and time, to a ninja, one of the legendary assassins from the far side of the past. She

---

*An apostrophe indicates use of the glottal stop ('Alif/Arabic) which is used in the local dialect of Teragon.

wore a loose, pajamalike garment of dull black. Her face had been carefully blackened out.

Demsing started to draw away, motivated by the waves of fear-substance the thing was emitting at him. All the data he could get from this event, directly, had registered. There was no more to be done. It was a shame, he thought; the girl was slender and childlike, with a face which under other circumstances might be described as elfin and lovely. The lines of her face betrayed the soft blurred features of youth.

Her training at the School would have involved, as a matter of course, not only the mastery of martial arts, dance, and gymnastics, but techniques of seduction and sexual performances. Taken at birth, selectees were taught to swim while still suckling babes. She would be skilled in the use of internal muscles, and now that skill and control would, under the stresses induced by the plant, start tearing her internal organs loose within a matter of hours. It was doubtful she would live more than a standard day, even with the plant helping to keep her alive.

He also knew he would have to leave this place quickly, before he could be discovered by the flunkies of the Tong. Demsing stepped back, leaving, when he heard an almost inaudible sound from the girl, an inhuman sound that made the back of his neck prickle and his bladder weak. He turned back to the girl, moved close to her.

She had, with incredible effort, brought her head forward; her mouth was still open, slack, and saliva ran from one corner. Sweat stained her clothing and ran down her forehead into her eyes. Her eyes were still glassy, focused upon some internal hellish panorama only she could imagine, a *she'ol* of unendurable pleasure indefinitely prolonged. But somehow she had called on all of her resources and was using them now. It seemed that she could see him, dimly, part of the time. She seemed to flicker in and out of consciousness.

The lovely, blurred mouth worked, tried to shape words, and at last forced out, in a faint hoarse whisper broken by involuntary whimpers and catches, ". . . can't stand it. Give me . . ."

Demsing drew his knife. "Who are you? Why follow me?"

". . . ah! Can't die. . . ." Her head fell back and her body moved in the throes of some deep inner convulsion. Her eyes focused on him again. ". . . years . . . inside here. Torn inside . . . die. . . . can't . . . you won . . . kill me . . ."

He felt beside her left breast for the heart, which was now beating rapidly. He readied himself for the thrust. "Why?"

She groaned out, infinitely slowly, ". . . Vollbrecht . . . do it now. . . ."

Her eyes rolled back into her head alarmingly until only the whites showed, and her voice made a low throbbing sound, an animal noise Demsing could not interpret. When her head came back to near-normal, and her eyes returned, the eyes faced in different directions and moved independently. She repeated, ". . . Vollbrecht . . . . . . please . . . now . . ."

Demsing began to hear sounds from the far side

of the Garden: he had just enough time. He thrust in the knife, and felt her heart jump violently on it. Her body made one last powerful contraction, releasing her bladder and bowels in the reaction of death.

The Carrionflower seemed hardly to notice. After the initial relaxation, the contractions began again, although at a much-reduced strength and rate. The plant was now maintaining her body systems independently, and could prolong her as a chemical factory for its needs for several more hours. Left alone, it would eventually consume the entire body.

Demsing did not wait, but faded to the wall and slid up it like a shadow, only seconds ahead of the Tong flunkies.

On Teragon, as everywhere else, whether its inhabitants knew it or not, information did not merely represent power, it *was* power. Therefore after leaving the neighborhood of the Tong, Demsing carefully thought over what he had just seen, because in this there was the unmistakable flow of the powerful currents of real and hard information. So who knew it, and how soon? And information was even more perishable than food.

To be followed, briefly, occasionally, or even habitually, was neither unusual nor alarming for most of the inhabitants of Teragon. But in this case, because of who had been following, and because of the unusual persistence she had displayed, even to the point of becoming captured by a Carrionflower, the act was exceptional and definitely worth examination. The surveillance had been paid for, and it had not been cheap, which implied the attention of real powers on Teragon which Demsing did not wish aroused or alerted.

His mission this night had been in his view of negligible importance, or at least so he had calculated it: a minor arrangement of negotiation between an obscure neighborhood sovyet and the metallists' Syndic. The matter had been so routine that he had considered it worthy of lesser diplos, and had almost not taken it. So now he reconsidered the task in the new light.

And arrived at no new conclusions. The job had been minor-league, and remained so on second and third examinations. Therefore the shadow had been on him, and not on the job. And so who had paid, and for what purpose? The neighborhood sovyet couldn't afford a *kobith*, and the Metallists were too tight to pay.

Then he considered the girl. For a moment, Demsing felt regrets at having killed her. But she had begged for it. And besides, victims of Carrionflowers needed considerable care; her own people wouldn't have provided it, because *kobith* were sent out absolutely on their own. That was their code. And he had no place to keep such a girl. And of course the beauty was a carefully selected illusion. No more dangerous or independent an adversary could be found. It would be equivalent to attempting to heal a wild animal. And that, too, was part of Teragon: no one took in strays, and need was the most bottomless pit of all.

She had walked into a Carrionflower trap. Obviously, she could be expected to know about such things, and to be thoroughly trained to resist them, so why she did so required some thinking out. He had not recognized her for what she was until after she was caught; before that, the only impression he had had of her was that she was good at her work, definitely in the upper orders. He thought wryly that had he known she was a *Kobith*, he would not have tried the Carrionflower stunt; he would have expected her to walk right past it. This was a piece with a loose end he couldn't tie down. She should not have failed.

A long shot was the possibility that she had intended to fail, which fit in with himself being the target. But that, in turn, suggested an accuracy of assessment of his own capabilities which he seriously doubted anyone competent to make: Demsing had learned early to keep his mouth shut and had not survived as a free agent into his middle thirties standard by opening it—or, equally important, allowing any assessments of his ability to be revealed. Still, that was a possibility and it needed evaluating in its turn. And if she had been the target, then there was a reason for that, too. But that didn't concern him. It could have been a thousand things—one of their arcane and ironic punishments for some imaginary transgression. Still, it made him uncomfortable, and for that, he needed to make some tests over the next few days.

And of course, the only data she had given him: Vollbrecht. She knew like everyone else on this world that no one got anything for nothing, not even death, and so, with the superhuman reserves of her class, she had broken all her vows and given him something in exchange for the service of releasing her from the plant. "Vollbrecht." He rolled the word over in his mind. A who or a what? And as he expected, it was a loaded gift: asking questions carelessly about "Vollbrecht" could be the most foolhardy thing he'd ever done. Still, he had subtle ways of teasing information out of his planet.

Lastly, there was the problem of the "scene" the plant's hallucinogens had evoked; not an image from memory, but something alien and strange. A memory not his own. This was not the first time such a flashback had occurred to him, but it was the first in which the gender crossover had been so clear and well-defined. Perhaps the presence of the girl had confused the plant's feedback chemistry, and that had manufactured a response out of nothing. And the plant, sensing it had two, had stepped up the concentration to compensate. Certainly that blast at the end had been overwhelming. But something remained, even after that careful hypothesis: it was part of the known rules of the game that Carrionflower hallucinations always involved memory.

Unlike the other questions he had, this last one gave him no access to Teragon's plots within plots, the games within games, *indeed some played for their own sake and no other goal.* This last question could be the most dangerous question of all that had emerged from the events of this incident. Whom could he ask, except himself? And if that self answered, what would it say—or do?

Demsing filed this all away in his mind, in a system of priorities which he would return to until he had dug it all out, and then proceeded with his original mission, satisfied again that this time, there was no shadow on him. He checked his watch just before he entered the zone of the particular neighborhood sovyet, and smiled at himself and the night; even considering the delays, the Carrion-flower incident, and the incidental time he had used up, he was only running about an hour behind the original schedule, which was well within the tolerances of his contract.

2

We say of Fire that it's a good servant but a bad master, and that seems agreeable enough, and so everyone smiles at the 'folksy' expression. But what we don't see quite so easily is how that perception applies to all of the unique inventions of humanity, and most especially to Language. Language is so marvelous a tool that it seduces us into believing that something can exist merely because we may, at our pleasure, assign a name to an imaginary something, and then perform grammatical operations on that noun, just as if it were a symbol for an iron ball. Consider the word "levity," which used to describe a force opposing gravity, or "Coriolis Force," which isn't a force at all. Now consider "talent." This is a word which is heard daily. But there is no such thing as talent: it is as fraudulent as Piltdown Man, as erroneous as the Ether, and as dangerous as Lysenko's genetics, because it leads us to look for and anticipate a phantom belief. What does exist is a will to succeed through self-discipline, which is, as they say, a horse of an entirely different color.

H. C., Atropine 1984

Sa'andro preferred to refer to himself as a futures broker, but the futures which he served were, for the most part, illicit, even according to the habitual practices of Teragon. Occasionally, his activities bordered on conceptual regions for which there was no word denoting degree of criminality. These degrees were certainly as real and measurable as wavelengths of ultraviolet light, but as yet humans had not learned to assign color names to different parts of the spectrum. For these reasons, then, and because even at an advanced age and devoted to well-developed epicurean appetites, he was accorded great respect, and the confidentiality of his house was a byword. Sometimes coins, never highly valued on Teragon, were lent legitimacy by the redeemer claiming, "Sa'andro spit on this very coin!"*

It was for these very qualities that Demsing occasionally sought out The Fat Man. Sa'andro was also a reputable broker of hard information, especially on the subject of who wanted what for how much. He maintained his own network of informers and watchers, and made up the difference for using second-raters by enfolding them within a subtle and powerful organization.

The Fat Man himself kept mostly to the Meroe District, where he did not have to stir far, nor wait long, for his tidbits. He operated an old-fashioned teahouse as a front, displaying to idle passersby an

---

*"Money" on Teragon consisted of essentially private promissory notes issued by various organizations with wildly varying degrees of confidence and redeemability.

outdoor patio, an inner public room, a serving-bar, and an alcove where sometimes musicians played for the subtle approvals of their dour audience. The Fat Man himself presided in a room upstairs, enthroned on or within an ancient sofa reputed to have come from Earth itself with the original discoverers of Teragon, surrounded by paper and junk which transcended all of the ordinary uses of the words.

It was here, then, that Demsing would begin his search for the answers which fit subtle and dangerous questions; he wandered past the teahouse like a casual passerby, and hesitated before he went in, as if the thought had just occurred to him. Once inside, he drifted over to a booth near the musicians' alcove, requested a mug of the local brew, which he knew was not "tea" proper, but the leaves of the Yaupon, which grew well in the hydroponic gardens underground.

He waited; that was the way it normally worked. No one seemed to be watching overtly, but invariably whoever came in was duly noted and reported. Demsing frankly did not know exactly how it was done; presumably by a sophisticated gesture language of secret signs, the practice of which was a high art form. According to whom the visitor might be, various things might happen: a summons to the upper room, or, equally probable, an invitation to leave.

The musicians were filing in for their performance. Their *evening* performance, as it were, even though one could, with one's very eyes, look out the window and see Primary gliding across the dark indigo sky of Teragon.*

It happened that it was the bassist who carried the summons. As he passed, carrying his cumbersome but expressive instrument, he leaned over, as if to pass a pleasantry, and said, in a low voice, "The Fat Man knows you know the way."

Demsing said nothing, and stood up as if nothing had happened. There was no gratuity; it was an unwritten code that the sender of a message bore the cost of compensation. He tossed off the remainder of his tea, which was indeed bitter, but which lent a particular clarity to the senses, and strolled away from the booth, as leisurely as he had come in, and just as leisurely, turned at the bar, passed through a frayed flower-print curtain, and started up the narrow stairs to the upper room.

---

*Time on Teragon is synchronized with Interplanetary Standard Time, and ignores the local "day" of the planet as much as possible. Teragon, slightly smaller than Venus, orbits an FO white dwarf of about one solar mass at a distance of 17 million miles. The resultant "year" is 29 days long. However, Teragon itself rotates once in 13 Standard Hours, retrograde, and its axis of rotation intersects the plane of the orbit at an angle of 22 degrees, which gives an erratic "daylight" to the surface. In fact, the daylight is rather dim, barely strong enough to read by. Primary shows a small disk, larger than a planet, smaller than a moon, an intense off-white, chalky glare, dangerous to stare at, which casts razor-sharp shadows.

The planet does not receive enough heat from Primary to sustain life or habitable temperature, so the contribution of Primary is negligible. The planet's heat comes from careful and sophisticated controls of the energy waste of its civilization.

Teragon, although deep in a steep gravity well, does not exhibit noticeable tidal phenomena.

He wondered how the Fat Man negotiated these stairs: they were damnably narrow, and the riser tread was burglar-steep, these stairs an effort even for the best. Demsing smiled faintly at the message this perception conveyed: *the stairs are obviously too easy to defend or block entirely. Therefore the Fat Man never uses this passage. This is only for permitted approaches, not interceptions.* Demsing constantly read the environment around him, noting placements, patterns, obvious statements and some not so obvious.

At the top of the stair, the upper room was much as he had seen it before: piles of paper everywhere, in untidy stacks which overflowed onto the floor. The Fat Man sat on his sofa as if he'd grown into it, sweating with the sustained effort of holding his bulk up in a sitting position. With him, sitting on a hard chair in the corner, was a sharp-faced little rat of a fellow Demsing guessed might be sixty standard years old, thin, short, intense. That one bore the look of having been abused often, from an early date. He constantly glanced around, all over the room, as if at any moment he expected to see an army of centipedes erupting out of one of the cracks in the ancient masonry. Meroe was an old section.

Sa'andro spoke in a soft basso rumble which had the peculiar property of projecting with virtually no sensible volume, nor could a hearer determine from where he spoke; it seemed to emanate from the very walls. He said, "I am very happy to see you, Demsing." (He breathed hard in pauses between words and phrases.) "The Metallists' Syn-

dic was most pleased with the arrangements you
helped them firm up. I told Horga, their rep, that
those kinds of things followed naturally when one
took the time to hire the services of the best."

Demsing flinched inwardly; he knew that a conversation which began with compliments could
not but lead to more requests for even more services, some of them probably exotic, indeed. Perhaps he had allowed himself to become slack by
stopping by here as much as he did, which in the
abstract wasn't all that often. There were others
besides Sa'andro.

As if divining part of his thought, Sa'andro
panted and mused, "Certainly, there was a time
when we saw more of you than we do now."

Demsing said, plainly, but respectfully, "One
thing leads to another; some of the contacts I
make with your aid sometimes ask for additional
services." He paused a moment, and then added,
"I always mention royalties and the courtesies of
the trade."

"Of course, my friend! And would you believe
that they also ratify their sentiments with definite
quid-pro-quos! Absolutely marvelous in the context of an age in which one has to send out a small
army to collect debits which, in my day, were paid
out of pocket receipts. No, indeed, not a word of
odious reproof; by far, you have the best repute of
all my independents. More than once I have spec-
ulated, I have daydreamed, what it might be like
to have the better of my bondsmen study under
you, learn your methodology . . . but I also suspect

that this is a hopeless, unrequited situation in which I might ever be the wishful suitor."*

Demsing thought through his own answer carefully before committing it to words. After a moment, he said, "It is true that I used to take some in, sporadically, and that I do not, currently. The reason is that not enough of them work out. There is some waste in the process. I found I could not in truth offer the genuine article to group operators, without a severe price in manpower which none of them would wish to pay. Such a course would in time become highly counterproductive."

"Would there not be a cure for this? Could one be found?"

Demsing said, "Possibly. It would be beyond the scope of my operations, and probably beyond that of most group operators to search it out and perfect it. Realistically, your own operators seem to do well enough for the goals you set them to."

"That is true, but one has to watch them so closely. . . . In your opinion, do other group operators have the same problem?"

"All groups share this to lesser or greater extent.

---

*The speech of Teragon is full of allusions and elliptical constructions because it is carefully attempting to obtain information without giving any away, or at best, to maintain the best ratio between the two functions. It is the habit of natives to extract information from a questioner by careful analysis of the questions; therefore, persons who have legitimate questions or exploratory probes will cloak them in extremely tactful constructions or else cast misleading or muddying implied sources. In this particular case, Sa'andro represented himself as a romantic suitor, as if admiring a beauty from a distance, which is without question a case of false flattery.

It is a function of group operations. For some, it is a severe problem; for others, it's a minor irritant. One has to have a good structure, and one also has to match the agents and their capabilities against realistic goals. Such systems seem to work well enough. I would, candidly, rate your organization as one of the better ones. But of course it exhibits the features I mentioned."

"Stroke for stroke, dear Demsing, that is why I ask for your company! But the price I have to pay for that . . . you would not imagine! But you have given me useful information and I will trade for that."

Demsing shifted the subject. "You have heard of peculiar events in conjunction with my most recent stunt?"

Sa'andro made pursing motions with his enormous lips which moved masses of gristle over the sweating face. For a long time, the Fat Man said nothing, but eventually, words rumbled out: "I have heard a persistent rumor to the effect that the Order of Sisters of Our Lady of Mercy would be very interested in ascertaining how one of their best novices came to reside in the embrace of a Carrionflower."

Demsing answered, agreeably, smiling, "Sometimes hard and dependable answers are very costly."

"Oh, they are aware of the cost, you may be certain."

Demsing said nothing, implying that he thought the Fat Man hadn't completed his thought, which would help him say more. He thought Sa'andro could see through that, but if the other did, he gave no sign of it, which was damn good control. After a pause, he continued speaking.

"There was something of an issue over it. The Sisters are currently embroiled in controversy with the Llai Tong as a result. Other than that and the fancy footwork on both parts, we have been able to recover nothing—not concrete, not hints."

"Then they aren't talking."

"My boy, they don't even talk about routine things: that is precisely why they are who they are. They start with the basics: I *expect* it of them."

Demsing mused, "One might speculate on the subject of revenge."

"Who among us has no enemies? But there seems to be no reflection of that whatsoever. That might itself tell a lot."

"It might tell me ... that my shadow was paid for so highly in advance that the loss was negligible by comparison, or that the mission was so trivial that the loss was, from my position, equally negligible. I should disqualify the latter."

"I had similar thoughts."

"Well, one can't live in a hole, can one?"

Sa'andro agreed, "No. And now allow me to introduce my friend, who has been here all along. I am a poor host." He nodded toward the small, thin man. "This will be Urst, who is my Archive. Not many have met him, but his reach is far and we have been friends and comrades in adventure for a long time, as time goes on this world."

Demsing nodded to the thin man, Urst, acknowledging him. He understood immediately the importance of what he was being shown. The descriptive terms for such a person as Urst were almost as numerous as their personal names, but they all meant the same thing in function: one who collected facts and connected them, and made that up into a map, and made sense of that map for their masters. Where did such types come from? He thought that perhaps they arose in the streets as sharpers who watched intently from the sidelines, but who lacked the will and nerve to engage themselves directly. Such men and women became gossips and idle tale-bearers on worlds of less-essential realities; here, they made themselves useful to emerging leaders who didn't know much but who possessed an excess of nerve. Once that connection had been made and proven with demonstrable success, they would withdraw into the shadows they loved, fed with selected tasks and provided information from the streets. And if they survived, they would become something more than slaves—and something less than fully formed individuals. It might be proper to describe them as extensions of their masters; so much so that few of them survived the loss of a master. They were hated and feared, with justification.

They were also kept away from the direct dealings of their masters, under the doctrine that "excessive exposure of Minds to direct operational matters clouded their insights." And empirical history, such as was generally known, tended to bear this view out.

So for Sa'andro to show Urst to him certainly carried meaning far beyond what was immediately apparent. *The truth was that Sa'andro was showing Demsing to Urst, not vice-versa. And that in turn meant that the Archive's assessment in situ was crucial for something which Sa'andro or Urst had in mind.*

Like the compliment with which Sa'andro had opened the meeting, this was also a most loaded gift. And he saw that neither of them cared if he saw this, as he certainly did. In fact, they wanted him to see it: that was the piece they were waiting for.

Demsing asked, "Do I fit the projections?"

Urst answered, speaking to Sa'andro, "Use him."

Sa'andro sighed deeply, quivering his pendulous jowls, and extracted a scented handkerchief to mop his brow. Demsing wondered at that: it was a bit chilly now, really too cool for sweating, so something was indeed balanced precariously here.

The Fat Man began, "In the past, I have acted as a broker for a small and select group of independent operators, and for my own ... ah, personal ventures, I used my own people."

Demsing agreed, "Yes, that is true."

"I have a matter to advance which is most confidential. In fact, not to be rude, but I would have to have your service guaranteed before I could bring such a thing up. There would be penalty clauses, of course."

"Of course."

"How would you feel about such a proposal?"

Demsing appeared to stop and think deeply for a moment, which was solely for effect. The moment was now. He ruminated, "You know that to the independent agent, his or her independence of operation is the single thing that enables him to operate in some of the areas he might have to visit. So, if I, for example, were to enter a restricted service agreement with a given operator, I would lose that part of myself which is most for sale."

"For a time!"

"You probably know better than I, how these things work. In this case, 'for a time' means forever. Others use mindsmen; they hear, they see, they expand and project data. So others would know. As an independent, I can serve operators who would become the untouchable enemy within someone's specific service. Understand, I am not one to shy away from hard work—what's needed; but these things breed vendettas and that's bad for all of us."

Sa'andro leaned forward, puffing, "Such things do not go unknown—nor uncompensated. I am aware of the independent's stock in trade and how much I would be taking." He added, peevishly, "Everyone knows I pay too much!"

Demsing thought, *Whatever it is, it's big and that's certain.* The Fat Man never haggled, and yet here he was, suggesting he would, and then some more. Demsing said, "How much?"

"You do the stunt, and then it's semi-retired protected immunity. You train my troops."

The offer was substantial. It meant, in effect, guaranteed income for life, and within reason, anything you wanted. And Demsing knew how much "anything" meant on Teragon. And protection, too!

This had to be something so big and so radical that Sa'andro wouldn't dare try it with his own people, and he wouldn't put it out for contract for fear of having it get out. But there was the price—you had to pay to hear what it was.

He said, "That's a lot. But remember, I'd be giving up a life I'd worked long to build—and giving up the chance to start my own operation up someday." This was standard independent idle talk, something every agent claimed to want. And few attained.

Sa'andro said nothing.

Demsing added, "Based on what I know at this moment, I would have to rate this as a risk greater than I'd care to take, as presented. It's not that I want to know more; just that without something concrete in advance. . . ."

Sa'andro squinted hard at him, his eyes becoming porcine and dangerously feral. The Fat Man glanced swiftly at Urst, and then rumbled in a sub-basso even deeper than the tones he'd used before, "All right, I'll give you three wishes of Urst: ask him anything! Then you serve!"

Demsing countered, "One question, not pertaining to this operation under discussion, bonded confidentiality both sides, and the freedom to say yes or no. I have a question, and I'll risk that. According to the answer I get."

"According to the answer?" Sa'andro sat back, making small blowing motions with his lips. "That puts me out in the cold, blind and naked with a target painted on my arse."

Demsing: "If his answer isn't enough, then you

can't protect me no matter what you think your organization can do." This was hard bargaining, the hardest he'd ever attempted with the Fat Man. And win, lose, or draw, something permanent was changing right now in this room whether he liked it or not. There were some transactions that changed things, to where there was no return to *status quo ante bellum.* No return. A lot of transactions were that way, but some were subtle. No one could miss this. He thought, *Well—one adapts. I have survived sometimes because I assigned changer status to what others thought were trivial events.*

Sa'andro hesitated just long enough for Demsing to see easily and clearly that the pause was entirely theatrical. Then, he breathed, wearily, "Done. Ask it!"

Demsing turned to the mindsman, Urst. "Tell me about Vollbrecht." Then he added, "Free association."

Urst registered neither surprise nor recognition, which was the expected response. Mindsmen learned poker-faces early on. What was unexpected was the reply: "I have nothing on a Vollbrecht of any sort. Give me a key: what is it? A person, an organization, what?"

"You know *nothing?*"

"I have never heard the name in any context."

Sa'andro settled his unruly bulk back into the recesses of the smelly sofa, and Demsing realized how tense the Fat Man had been. And the gambit had failed for both of them. Dead end. But there was one datum here: Whatever it was, the Fat Man was not in on it. He asked, "Restricted data?"

Sa'andro said, "Tell the truth. It's blown, anyway."

Urst said, quietly, "Truth: nothing."

Demsing shrugged, and sighed, "You can't protect me better than I can myself. So whatever your project is, I am better off to pass. But I understand what a resource I used, and so in trade I offer you one contract stunt for another operator at no charge to you. I can at least show some gratitude."

The Fat Man asked, softly, "Is Vollbrecht your enemy?"

Demsing started to say yes, but something stopped him. Not necessarily what that might reveal to this dangerous broker of arrangements, but in truth, something deep in his mind told him that he really did not know the answer to that question. He said, "I don't know that at this point. It is something I am working on, and before I proceed along that line of development any further, I should determine what Vollbrecht is."

"But it could be your enemy?"

"That is certainly possible."

Sa'andro nodded and rumbled, " 'Probable,' for the cautious man. Very well: I will consider the stunt offer. As for the present, I have nothing immediately suitable."

And Demsing understood that, too. It meant, clearly enough, that he was being cut off because of his asking price. But all things considered, it was probably better that he left Sa'andro for a time. Certainly he did not want to be involved in a radical operation that failed. Such things left a lot of wreckage behind and not infrequently sucked in good agents as well.

Sa'andro had revealed a lot. But Demsing had revealed a name of interest, too. Yes. It was time to fade out of this sector of Teragon. Bond or not, Sa'andro would be looking for a buyer for that piece of data before Demsing had cleared the teahouse. The relationship had become uncomfortable.

In fact, the relationship had become dangerous. And as if the very walls had read the minds within the room, a fourth man entered the room behind Sa'andro, from a concealed passage. Demsing recognized the type instantly, and understood how fast things had decayed here. The fourth man was young, of graceful, lean build, muscular but not excessively so. Here was no independent agent, to take on any assignment and expect to average out ahead on one's wits, but rather a narrow-specialist who was uncontestably superior in one thing and useless in all others. This would be a bodyguard who was highly specialized and tuned to small, enclosed spaces, and close combat. Demsing had confidence in his own abilities, but prudence was part of his repertory as well, and he did not as a rule take on specialists in their own proper environments.

They knew he would see that. The bodyguard wasn't so much an open threat, as the cover of an avenue of action. They were telling him he'd have to leave with the risks as they were, intact. On both sides.

Demsing nodded politely to the newcomer, and

stood, very relaxed, turning to go. He said, "I should leave. I have another contact I had scheduled. . . ."

Sa'andro rumbled, pleasantly, "You would not stay for dinner? One of my clients owes me a dinner as a debt, and as it happens, he has obtained a fine cook in his employ who makes a fine and authentic couscous. . . ."

"Perhaps another time, if the invitation is a standing one."

The Fat Man wobbled his head in agreement. "Yes, just so. Ahem, but our times have become so hasty. Yes, that is the word: hasty. I wish there were more time for the little amenities."

"You would probably be surprised to hear that many of my colleagues also feel that way, even as events press them into courses which might be considered 'hasty.' Still, what is one to do?"

Sa'andro waved his hand, as if shooing away an insect, fastidiously. "Certainly, certainly. But come again! Often, in fact: my house is yours!"

"Great regrets."

"Indeed, regrets. But good hunting to you!"

With that ending to their conversation, Demsing left the cluttered upper room and returned to the public room of the teahouse by the narrow stairs. When he reached the main room, the musicians were still playing, and Demsing took a mug from the counter and paused to listen to their progress through the complexities of an interminable song. The music of Teragon was based upon a system of improvisation within a broad harmonic and rhythmic framework which seemingly allowed almost anything, so long as it was done well and with style. This lent the music a strange, haunting quality, one always full of surprises.

He had also stopped to listen because it was unexpected. Upstairs now, they would expect him to hit the street running. But he knew he couldn't outrun street rumor, nor a comcircuit connection. So he waited, and smiled to himself at the thought of how much consternation and confusion this pause would be causing, and how many estimations and predictions were being re-evaluated.

The Bassist was playing an acoustic bass guitar, five-stringed and fretless, of course; now in the song, he took up his solo part, taking the implied melody and the rhythmic pattern and moving with them in the ways in which a windsailor might use the wind, steering a varied course only he knew, but in constant reference to the unseen wind. He did not land on each note, so much as he sidled into each one, sliding the notes from above and below and bending the heavy strings as well, and damping the notes with the palm of his right hand. The solo went smooth, like warm oil.

Demsing put down the mug. Now it was time to go, time to lose the inevitable shadow Sa'andro would put on him, at least for a while. He knew very well that the Fat Man wouldn't expect his own people to keep up with him for very long, but it was worth doing for as long as they could. Perhaps they thought they would derive something from the reports.

He stepped outside now, into the street, narrow and winding, with low buildings decorated with eccentric cupolas and bays hanging out over the street. It was T-night, now: Primary had sailed off somewhere behind the planet. Demsing set off easily and openly down the street, generally in the direction of the Fa'am District, walking easily as if he had all the time in the universe.

So much the watchers reported as well. They continued their reports for a considerable time, until one of them reported back that the target had vanished somewhere in the neighborhood of Aume's brothel, and was nowhere to be found. Sa'andro waved his hands in the air in dismay, Urst shrugged noncommitally. Aume was their own man, on their own street. One wouldn't think an outsider could find a way; but with Demsing, one had to expect the unexpected. Surprises.

As routine, they had all their field men check their territories, but of course, there was no report. Demsing had simply vanished.

Sa'andro finished his meal, wiped his face and told Urst, "Find out what this Vollbrecht is, and his connection with it."

Urst nodded, and excused himself. After a time he reported back, and his report was negative.

3

The attraction of the SF story is that it essentially happens somewhere else or somewhen else. We do not read it to find out what the Joneses are doing in Peoria or why things are the way they are in China. And that's fine: to read for adventure and visits to imaginary places is, for the most part, good for the soul. But you must always keep in mind that the very strangeness that you the reader enjoy so much is almost never perceived by the characters of the story itself. For them, to the contrary, the environment of the story is Home—familiar, everyday, ordinary, accepted without question, boring, exhilarating or terrifying to the same degrees and for the same reasons that our world is all those things to us in our turn. It is also good to recall that all fiction is elaboration of selected simplifications; this is why truth is stranger than fiction. Read the paper. So keep that borderline in mind; for if they, the characters, could see across it the way we see into their world, they'd think they were looking into an interplanetary zoo.

H. C., Atropine 1984

Now Demsing moved across the face of Teragon on one of its two long-range systems. Sometimes he was deep underground, but it was under only in the sense of being under the apparent roots of the buildings above. Teragon was like a tropical forest that way. There was no real surface—just deeper and deeper roots, becoming more tangled and intertwined the farther one went down. Sometimes he passed among places near or on the surface, riding in a singles compartment, watching the districts move past him in the artificially lit days and nights of the planet. Sometimes where the track went deep between areas, the shadows cast by the floodlights overhead were sharper than the shadows cast by Primary. *But Primary's shadows moved.* Constantly. Never still. And sometimes the track ran along elevated runways supported on pylons far above areas, the endless city passing beneath, a magic soft lumpy organic growth in the starlight fading to the black horizon.

Most people hated and avoided travel on Teragon, because it was disturbing in ways they had few defenses against. No effort had been made to make it pleasurable or entertaining: bodies were *freight*, and so the idea of travel was a functional and severely ascetic experience, designed so to discourage idle wandering. Idle wanderers saw things they did not understand, and began to ask questions.

The two main long-distance lines were neither speedy nor direct, but were labyrinthine and vinous fractal entanglements which spread over the planet like roots, like tentacles, narrow little roadways powered by a linear induction system which drove coupled strings of soft-tired drays.

There were no ships: no open water. There were

no aircraft: the atmosphere thinned too abruptly, and there was no open land upon which to build runways. Orbital vehicles were considered irrelevant. Nothing but the Linduc Roadways, with their strings of rounded, clumsy drays trundling along them at a steady speed of fifty kilometers an hour, headless trains of sausages bumping along in the twilight.

Demsing had come a great distance around the planet, far enough to put Sa'andro out of reach. Moving on was nothing new to him; he moved frequently, often shifting operating areas completely around the planet for no reasons at all, or else expressing rationalizations which he knew were nonsense even as he voiced them. The real reason was that he perceived more clearly as a stranger; events and patterns were not clouded by the fog of associations. And that he used the long and arduous journeys to clear his mind of a sort of dust, cobwebs and general untidiness which it seemed to collect from remaining in a smaller area for too long. It was a way of not simply becoming nobody, but of reaching beyond that for nothingness.

Long ago, he had understood, directly, without climbing an abstraction ladder to reach it, that thinking and dreaming were similar states of mind, closely related, both equally distant from the true state of the universe. It followed easily that if you could wake up from dreaming, you could also wake up from thinking, reaching a state of mind which somehow eluded Time, an Aorist kind of tense, unbounded, unlimited. *To think was to step out of the flow, and to lodge against dead monuments to the past.* To think was equivalent to attempting to retain a dream. It didn't help: it made things worse and more muddied.

He had often tried to pass this Aorist state on to others. Aorist Subjunctive. *What if?* But so far, he had not found one who could reach it. This disturbed one of his most basic assumptions, that everyone was basically similar and had similar abilities, if they would only reach for them, call on them. But they never did—or could. It eluded him, slid away. He saw creation as unfinished, that all were still immersed in Creation itself, that it was not some mysterious event in the unreachable past, but still here, now. You could write it as you went, write in what you wanted; the only thing was that one had to perform odd little acts, in themselves often unimportant and meaningless, but which seemed to energize the intended written state-to-be.

Sometimes it involved doing odd things to people he didn't know and had no interest in. Sometimes these acts were, of themselves, cruelties; equally probable, they could also be inexplicable kindnesses. *The moral valence of the acts seemed to have no relationship whatsoever with the valence of the completed state.*

But he couldn't pass it on. There was a wrongness there, but he couldn't quite see it, even in the Aorist. Something was in the way. And the flashbacks, too. They were related in some way to this, but again, he could not get a clear sight on it. For a long time, this had been in the back of his mind. He had seen it long ago, but put it away, for there were more important things to do. But it had never gone away, and in fact, he had become more conscious of it as time had passed. Certain things came easy to him without reason; and yet other actions came normally, as if he were learning them just like everyone else. Those things did not add up. He had begun to consider that perhaps it might be time to explore that anomaly.

Demsing got off the Linduc six days later at a place with a small port called Desimetre. The port area was like many others scattered across the face of Teragon, a closely woven series of Linduc roadways, terminating in a warehouse quarter on the left and an insignificant junction climbing off to the right up a narrow cleft which divided what was called Desimetre.

Desimetre occupied the south slope, where it tumbled steeply down to the deepest part, where the Linduc line ran. North of the line was another district, Petroniu, which held an altogether different ambiance. He had remarked that fact often, but not questioned it: it seemed perfectly correct that the division between areas should be both insignificant and subtle, for that was indeed the way of things. Petroniu was impoverished, dark, dangerous, and dirty. Desimetre was none of those things. It was sometimes almost as if a sunlight which Teragon had never known illuminated Desimetre, despite the undeniable fact that the poor light of Primary fell on all alike, the rich and educated, the ignorant and the poor. And on vice and virtue, which assumed different meanings according to where you were.

The streets and lanes among the compounds and shops of Desimetre were subtly wider, the compounds a little more finished, and the shops were more open. More people were on the street, and their business seemed less furtive. Nobody *scuttled* here. It was considerably quieter than most districts and was viewed as somewhat of a retirement resort and an entry point for offworlders, infrequent though they were, who were of course totally unfamiliar with the protocols of Teragon.

It was also a place where he had the most contacts; most, and most trustworthy, for it was his own home district. Here was where he had started from. Not that Desimetre was easy: far from it. Demsing continually assessed the District as one of the hardest to work in, not because of the relaxation, but because powerful and subtle groups operated from there, and they saw to it that the atmosphere remained unchained. To Demsing, lower-class districts like Petroniu were much easier to work, because they were invariably controlled by more sophisticated forces outside them, and so their inhabitants never initiated, but simply reacted to stimuli delivered according to someone else's plans and designs.

His first contact, after some routine exercises to ensure he was not being observed by anyone, was with a woman called Klippisch, who operated a small group similar to the Fat Man's, but of much higher quality and of greatly reduced scope. Unlike the Fat Man, in far off Meroe, she operated without a front, which still impressed Demsing: and to continue to do so was proof positive of diplomacy raised to the level of a performing art. Also, unlike many operators, she maintained a positive apprenticeship program which spotted many excellent youngsters coming along and provided them with good and basic standards for their later lives. And thanks to Klippisch, most of them had later lives to benefit from.

When he walked into the old office she was still using, she was having an intricate discussion with two men, apparently her own people, concerning the training of a new group which had just come in; they were so involved in this matter that none of them paid any attention to him. They knew someone was there, but who was unimportant. Then Klippisch recognized him.

She made fists of both hands, arms akimbo, and leaned back in her chair, grinning broadly. She was a compact woman of middle years whose active life had left her as supple and sleek as an otter, and solid as a brick. Her hair was clipped off short, except in the very back, where a short queue hung down, and was iron-gray in color. Her face showed an intricate network of wrinkles, frown lines as well as laugh lines. She had powerful, muscular hands and forearms, and still participated in stunts personally, which not many chiefs did.

Klippish exclaimed, from her leaned-back position, "Well, well! A stranger in these parts!"

"A stranger's stranger! But greetings to you all."

"Wonderful to see you again, Demsing. You are well?"

"Fed and profitable."

"Do you remember Dossifey?" She indicated the younger of the two men. "Maybe not. He was coming in about the time you were leaving. And Galitzyn?" She indicated the other. "We had to replace old Betancourt, who unfortunately died, just like the old beezer." Betancourt had been her Mind in the old days.

Demsing nodded to the two. Dossifey volunteered, "I remember you, but you've changed some. Of course, so have we all!" He chuckled to himself.

Klippisch cocked her left eye and asked, "Are you looking for work? I always have room."

"I wasn't especially looking, but if you need help, I'll do my part."

She nodded. "Need a place?"

"Wouldn't be a bad idea, actually."

She pursed her lips and said, "Dossifey can show you. Want to help out with some of the youngsters?"

"Fine. I've not worked with the kids for a long time."

"Well, well, what a find! We were just trying to figure out how we were going to get this bunch through, and in the door you stroll! What a day! Dossifey, go over to the safe house and check out a place for Demsing, will you?"

Dossifey touched his forehead with his right knuckles, smiled, and departed. Galitzyn nodded, and also left. Then she stopped, as if collecting her wits and her usual calmness, and asked, "You visiting openly, or you want it quiet?"

"Quite, please, as always. I'm invisible most of the time, now."

"I thought you'd go that way. Good. No problem." She put both hands on the desk in front of her, interlocked her fingers, and cracked her knuckles with a powerful rippling motion. "I'll lay it out, what I know: I haven't heard a thing about you since that Chukchai business."

Demsing smiled, faintly. "That was a while back."

"I thought you'd been offworld."

"Why?"

"A ship came in a while back, and after a discreet interval, here you are. Convenient. It was the *Vitus Bering*, out of Novosantiago. They parked out in the trailing trojan and sent a lighter over full of people. Some went back, some stayed. We are tracking a couple of them, on contract. Some, we are using for tow-targets for the kids. The rest . . . God only knows."

"You only had contract on some of them?"

"Right. No one can keep track of everyone. These were the usual sorts we get every now and then: traders, old relatives back for a visit. A couple of unexplaineds, I think. . . . And you, you fox, you could have sleazed right in there with them."

Demsing took a chair and slid into it. "Might have."

"Tell me nothing! I wish no knowledge of the beastly offworlds! Such a thing would distort my concentration."

"I also wish to know nothing."

"Then we shall make a fine pair . . ." She let it trail off.

Demsing asked, "Does my mother still live in Desimetre?"

"Faren? Indeed she does! Want to see her? I know she'd like to see you."

"What's she doing now?"

"Pipe inspection and repair for the Water Cabal, checking for sneaks and tappers and the like, and good at it, too. She's not in tip-top shape, of course, but considering her age, doing well enough. Age ... you know, the one thing we don't have here is geriatrics, so we're all back to square one with the old three-score and ten business. Still, I wouldn't have it any other way. I can tell her ..."

"Tell her I'm around. Presently, I'll stop by."

"You heard about Dorje?"

"Yes."

"Condolences. You're not here about that, are you?"

"No. I heard sometime back he'd been killed, before.... Just before. I had some of my contacts look into it. There was nothing I could have done, and nothing I should do now. You know I wasn't born of them, but adopted offworld. We all came from somewhere else. I learned...."

"Indeed you did. Abnormally fast, I should say!"

"... Faren learned. She'd been a smuggler. Dorje ... he did well enough, but there was always something in him that wouldn't change. He was in Enforcement before, and I think that he never adapted to the concept here of private enforcement and negotiated settlements."

"Yes," Klippisch said, slowly. "Out there, they think we are totally lawless, wild animals living in the ruins like rats."

Demsing smiled. "Pretty civilized, when you think about it."

"Wouldn't have it any other way. When I think about all those poor slogs out there in the dark beyond poor Primary, busting their arses for a gold chronograph with fourteen time zones of fifteen planets on it, a pat on the back, a kick in the toufass . . . no way!"

Demsing chuckled, "You should take a vacation out there, just to look at the natives!"

"Not me! Imagine having a sun that gave out real light and heat! Imagine! There you'd be, out in the open, with that goddamn bright *thing* glaring over your shoulder all day long . . . I hear some of those places have longer daylights than one of our whole days. Awful!"

"How are things, otherwise?"

"If the truth be told, a little quiet for my taste. It's been that way for a while, and of course nobody really wants to upset it. We have plenty to do, mind, in other districts. But it's quiet, here."

Demsing reflected, "I could stand a little quiet."

Klippisch agreed, "Everyone should slack off now and then. If you stayed up and alert all the time, you'd go fraggo, and if you slacked constantly, you'd be bored and starve. No solution but to mix them in proper order."

"I think I'll stay around for a time. But mind who knows I'm here, in Desimetre."

"Oh, for a certainty! We're as silent as the Sphinx, here."

"Did you really not know I had come?"

Klippisch looked at him sharply. "No, as a fact.

Slipped by me again. And as far as I know, you very well could have stepped off the *Vitus Bering*. Whatever it was, I don't want to know."

"I may have some questions for the net, if I may. I'll trade some current from the other parts for it."

"Are you working on some private thing?"

"Just a little insurance, so to speak."

Demsing spent the next few standard days re-learning Klippisch's routines and meeting her key people. The routines were as intricate and cautious as he remembered them, and the people, as he expected, were, to a man and woman, long on performance and short on ego. They seemed to work together easily and noiselessly without the need for excessive reflections of themselves in the eyes of others.

The main characters he saw the most of were Dossifey, who looked intense, with a hard, muscular frame and craggy good looks, but who wasn't, but was instead relaxed and placid, almost lazy, except for an uncanny skill he seemed to have cultivated to be in the right place in the right position at the right time. He made it look effortless, like all good artists, but the reality of it was that it was a lifelong discipline and he simply had never had time for anything else.

There was also a young woman, Thelledy, who looked like an attractive bit of fluff, but who certainly could not be, and who seemed to specialize in disappearing while one wasn't looking. Demsing caught glimpses of her, met her in short, chance meetings, and understood that without directed intent, he was not likely to see much more of her than that. As far as what she actually did in the organization, he could not quite see it, without devoting considerable effort to it.

The Mind, Galitzyn, was considerably more accessible than most of the cases he had seen, and certainly not evasive or apparently fuddled, as Demsing remembered the old Mind, Betancourt. Like many Minds, however, he was thin and underdeveloped, a middle-aged nonentity who scarcely bothered to conceal addictive vices which they all seemd to have in one form or another.

He spent his time divided between working with the youngsters in conjunction with Dossifey, who seemed to be in charge of that part of the operation, and with Galitzyn, who responded to patient questioning provided he was fed information in turn, and who brought Demsing gradually up to date on the general state of affairs in and around Desimetre, and what, in very general terms, the Klippisch Group was working on currently.

One of the items he traded Galitzyn concerned the increasing usage of computers in some of the Groups he had had contact with, a fact which seemed to rouse the old man out of his vulturine absorption.

"*Computers*, now, is it?"

"Paper Fan Group was further into that than anyone I saw, but I heard some talk there were others even further in. Even to the point of allowing Minds to erode themselves out of existence."

"Where you were, how do the others react to that?"

"Some fear it, that it gives the users an edge; others want the same thing because they think it's the thing to do. A minority are ignoring the whole thing."

Galitzyn growled, "The ones who ignore it will be the operations still in existence for the next generation."

"Why so?"

"Don't you think that's been done before? A thousand times on a thousand worlds! It's a failure of nerve, that's all." He stopped, as if the subject were one he did not dare give full expression to. He said, after a moment in which he had tried to sum up the essentially unsummable, "The problem isn't with the machines, but with the abuse of usage that the people fall into. Basically, this is a variation of the weapons argument, from the most ancient days of which we can have record. What things like this do is expand the reach of idiots and cretins, which allows a clumsiness and a lack of foresight and goals to swamp the efforts of better-trained people. Eventually, the contest slips over into a contest of firepower, or horsepower, or some other-power which fools can buy instead of building the capability into themselves. And what restores the balance? A sort of self-perception and will which has to be managed very carefully so that it itself does not become berserker-destructive. Initially, in a cycle like this, it seems to go all to the machine-users, but when a certain density is reached, then raiders chip it all away. People who are enraged beyond the controls of reason don't need guns, if it comes to it, nor knives. They have hands and teeth, if need be. I am sorry to hear of this, though; I thought we had all pretty well painted that corner over."

Demsing volunteered, "You see that trait in the apprentices: to take the short cuts, which in the end gloss over the key things you need to see yourself and handle."

"Exactly. Handle. That's the word."

"Can you use that information here?"

"Oh, yes. Indeed we can. Klip will want to start exploiting that weakness immediately. As I said, it's not the machine, but the use. We have methods of identifying that sort of abuse once we have reason to believe it exists. Very useful. So, now: you have given one, so you can take one."

"I have two, but one is more confirmation than anything else."

"One, two, what are numbers among associates? Honor among thieves, so to speak."

And by this, Demsing knew that the information he had carried was extremely valuable. That meant, with high probability, that one of their rival organizations had been displaying those, or similar traits. He asked, "The small one is about Carrion-flower poisoning."

"Go on."

"When they receive the chemical tracers of one's body chemistry, they emit a tuned scent to key into the recognition areas of the brain. My question is, do they evoke random images, or images stored in memory?"

"Easy enough: memory only. Gollehon did experiments with chained volunteers, in 3035 Standard, which demonstrated beyond doubt that a specific area of the brain was activated—a section which deals specifically with the recognition and meaningfulness of remembered faces and bodies. Sometimes it seems otherwise subjectively, but in every case, there was a memory linkage, however weak. No cases of the contrary have been cited. In this case, the official version resembles the popular one."

"What happens with multiple potential victims?"

"If the plant perceives the two as equal in strength, two or more, it selects a sex randomly, one or the other, and emits accordingly. If the multiple persons are predisposed toward one sex, it increases the dosage to increase the possibility one will approach close enough for capture. In the latter case, for the comparatively weaker individuals, the increased emission can be expected to overwhelm any defenses such a person might have. In this pattern, it operates, if that is the proper word, almost exactly like the classical predator: it takes the weakest, and it acts to heighten probabilities."

"Does anyone know where they originated?"

"Unknown. According to my information, Carrionflowers are found on several planets, evenly dispersed throughout the volume of the part of the Galaxy we know directly. In no case can they be demonstrated to be products of the native ecosystem."

"Someone should pursue this."

"Doubtless they should. There are, however, more questions at present than there are savants to answer them. Certainly there are more questions than answers, which is as it should be. The situation is basically unsolvable."

"That is number one. This will be two: Vollbrecht."

"That's all you have?"

"That's all. I don't know what it refers to."

"On the *Vitus Bering*'s passenger list, there was an entry for a person Pitalny Vollbrecht. That is all I have."

"Restricted?"

"No. We held no commission to track such a person, and did not. I can tell you that several untracked persons debarked here, and I can also tell you that the number who left was the same as those who came. I cannot tell you if those were precisely the same. Again, we held no such commission."

Demsing thought, wide awake, *But they did hold a commission to check the passenger list. Why? For whom? Somebody reported that information, and Galitzyn memorized it. Curious, indeed.* He observed Galitzyn closely, and detected signs of the beginning of agitation. Perhaps it would be best not to press him further, at least for now.

And what he had wasn't much. But it was something. He asked, "What sort of ship was the *Bering*?"

"Express packet." *A small ship.* "Outbound for the 47 Tucanae Cluster."

"That's a *long* way off!"

"Obviously someone wants to go there, or send something." Galitzyn was becoming impatient.

Demsing and Galitzyn parted, and Demsing was certain that the Mind would report to Klippisch what questions he had asked. There was no cure for that, either. But he had something.

4

The trees of the forest front make an excellent screen for activity or states of being behind them, and let this be understood metaphorically as well as actually, for there are many kinds of screens and camouflage. However, one may see through this screen by standing still and observing motion beyond the screen, or else moving, and observing what stands still beyond. In both cases, there is a difference of perspective-perceived motion, real or illusory, which enables the master of this art to see through the screen as if it had never been there. It may also be noted in this context that the use of screening practices for cover approaches identity as it approaches perfection of concealment. Or, an enemy who is perfectly concealed may be unable to extricate himself from the structure of concealment.

H. C., Atropine Extracts

There was something to Galitzyn's answers which rang out of tune; not enough to alarm, but noticeable. At first, Demsing could not quite perceive the wrong, even though he could sense its presence, so he let it go for the moment, but he did not forget it in the days that followed, as he integrated himself into the routines and functions of Klippisch's organization. Quite naturally, the small group of apprentices he took over represented the ones Thelledy and Dossifey wanted to get rid of; he accepted this without complaint. Demsing had ways of making them bloom, and he began bringing them out as soon as he could be sure he had decent security within his group.

There were four of them, as random a collection of street urchins as one could hope to pick up off the streets of the districts of Teragon: Weenix and Slezer were underfed, sallow emigrants from Petroniu, precociously streetwise and perilously unsubtle, boys of mid-adolescence. Fintry was an even younger lad from Desimetre who seemed to have no apparent virtues save an eagerness to please. The last was Chalmour, a hoydenish ragamuffin who claimed to be from the far side of The Palterie, the district immediately to the south. Chalmour was agile and adept, of indeterminate age, and although definitely female, somewhat uncertain of role.

She was clearly the oldest, but all of them were full of observations, rumors, tales and legends which Demsing sifted through patiently, never correcting errors, indeed, he acted convincingly as if he had never noticed them.

One fact emerged which was very interesting to Demsing. The Mind, Galitzyn, was of recent vintage; very recent, and none of them knew where he had come from, or how Klippisch had come to take him in. There was no contradiction among the four of them, who all predated the arrival of Galitzyn.

Dossifey, Demsing remembered, dimly, as an undefined young boy coming in as he had been leaving. He had had little contact with him, but it was enough to place him. And on this the tales of the four agreed as well. It was Thelledy where the stories broke down.

Weenix and Slezer credited her with supernatural powers without question. Fintry was the most recent, and knew her least well, however, he had once seen her in a secret conversation with Galitzyn, which had awed him to silence. Chalmour provided another interesting item, that Thelledy had been knowledgeable of certain sexual techniques and had attempted to teach her some of them, but had presently given up.

Demsing had, as a matter of course, seduced Chalmour early, or allowed himself to be seduced. The distinction was neither clear nor especially important. It was expected, and pleasant, and no one made any serious objection to it. Chalmour was enthusiastic and cooperative, but displayed no unusual skills or practices. How Demsing had learned about Thelledy was through a peculiar movement Chalmour had attempted to perform, which had not seemed one of her own instinctive responses. She had explained, "Thelledy tried to show me how to do that, but I could never quite get the feel of it. You must grade me for trying."

"Oh, yes! An 'A' for effort! At least!"

She lay with him in the small room in the safe

house, stretched across his chest, wrapped up in the rough blanket to keep the chill away.

Demsing asked, "Did Thelledy prefer girls?"

"Oh, no, at least not so you could tell. The boys in her group she whipped into line and the girls she terrorized."

"I can imagine."

"Weenix and Slezer were with Dossifey's group, but Fintry and I were in hers."

"Why did she give me you and Fintry?"

"Fintry, I think, was too young. He's new. We all help with him. As for me, I always came off well in all the exercises and techniques, but she wanted me to try certain things. . . . I never seemed to respond to her satisfaction."

"What kinds of things?"

"Well, sex things, all of them, close or far. Sometimes it was a way to look, or walk, or smile. I couldn't remember to do it right. Other things were closer to the bone, you know, but doing them always seemed to get in the way, and . . . ha, ha, I'd forget! I thought it was a big joke, extra stuff, something she was culty on, because she was a bit fanny about it."

"Fanatic?"

"She covered it well, but it was something deep, all right. She really believed in it. And she could do it, too, all of it. Her boys. . . . I don't think they were normal anymore. They took chances for her, and she always lost more than anyone else."

"Accidents in action."

"Yes. But she was new, and so we all figured

Klip' was trying her out. You have to expect some losses."

"I don't like losing students. Afterwards, that's different."

"Klip' was pleased with what she turned out. And they were pretty good!"

And nobody knew where she had come from, either.

And most interesting was the information, courtesy Chalmour, that Thelledy had gone out to meet the *Vitus Bering*, with two assistants, Boncle and Poulwart, who were both lost on operations shortly afterwards in Petroniu.

Presently, after she had talked on about everything under Primary and then some, Demsing had felt her muscles relax, her slender body settle closer, warm and girl-fragrant, and her breathing become deep and regular, and he was alone with a head ringing with sudden suspicions. It was the kind of thing he recognized with an inward smile: just out of reach logically, but also close enough to be suspicious. And he had one of his own methods of dealing with that level. He relaxed. Now was not the time. He settled more loosely around the young girl, and cradled her more than a little protectively; if what he suspected was even close to being true—verifiable and predictive—she was extremely. fortunate to have escaped Thelledy with her life. And she was too good to waste.

Desimetre was bounded on the north by the Linduc line, its marshalling yards, the cleft in which it ran, and beyond that, the dreary purlieus of

Petroniu. Southwards, the district climbed an apparent ridge which always seemed too steep for Teragon, for it had, as far as anyone had discovered to date, no natural topography whatsoever. Southwards, beyond the top of the rise, the tops of buildings descended slightly and faded off to the horizon without distinguishing feature. This area was called The Palterie, allegedly owing to its lack of desirable targets.

Eastwards, the rise dipped into a spoon-shaped depression called Shehir, a small and self-conscious enclave which had gone over almost entirely to a defensivist attitude and was currently suffering from an excess of security mercenaries, which had the end result of making the district even more vulnerable.

Westwards, there were two small districts, the one nearest to the Linduc line being a surface manifestation of the Water Cabal called Gueldres; and on the south side, shading off into The Palterie was an even smaller district called Ctameron, whose distinguishing feature seemed to be modest towers surfaced with a particularly smooth glaze.

These areas Demsing knew well, as well as he knew any part of Teragon; but even here, there was always change and one had to figure for it. Gueldres was considered a truce zone and little, if anything, went on there. Shehir had broken off from a section of Desimetre, and had gone severely downhill since. Ctameron seemed to be creeping slowly into The Palterie. Petroniu and The Palterie remained as they always had been, the one meaninglessly dark and malevolent, and the other equally meaninglessly light and threatless, although such terms were of course modified by the peculiar relativities of Teragon, where light and dark were sometimes hard to distinguish.

Now Demsing was alone, in his own place, a bare little room. They had sent the apprentices off on a short vacation, Klippisch advising them, "Enjoy the time. Soon, there will only be such Time as is stealable." Practicing their new skills, Demsing's group had appeared to hang around uncertainly, but when Klippisch looked for one of them to run a short errand, thinking perhaps that they were useless underfoot, she discovered to her surprise that all of them were gone, vanished without a trace, and that Thelledy's group were the ones still milling around. Klippisch looked sharply at Demsing, who met her eyes and pointedly turned away. But he watched Thelledy with his peripheral vision, never leaving her unobserved, and for an instant, something alien and hostile glared out of her eyes, something more emphatic than an outclassed group leader.

Yes. He remembered that. And other things, too, things he had been told, and things he had observed himself.

At times, he could call on something deeper within himself which he didn't entirely understand, a state of being he had no description for, and something which in truth he feared. It was never easy: he had to work at it, harder than anything he knew, and a specific kind of stress helped trigger it. It was a strange, contradictory path: he would sink deeper within his consciousness, but at the same time maintaining a tension, calling on himself to "wake up from thinking," to let go. And if he entered the state correctly, carefully, he could extrapolate predictable certainties from amazingly small fragmentary artifacts of reality, as he thought of them. Another thing happened to him: his perception of Time shifted radically.

Now Primary was slowing in its mad careen across the sky and hung in space, spinning deliberately, its enormous degenerate mass dangerously approaching absolute limits of Time and Space. Spinning. *Spinning!* He almost lost it when he saw that. Primary had enormous spin, left over, like its worthless heat, from the time when it had been a real star, fueled, running.

In this state he was a transit point for data, a junction on an intersection of infinite lines of communications. He saw everything, and everything could not be contained in the perception of a finite being, nor formed within the limits of linear language. He had to abandon Will, but he had to exercise it to select. Primary obsessed him, dominated him, and he blocked it out just as he blocked out the ramifications of the definition of a city, a junction point among lines of communications at which flows were shifted from one line to others. Teragon was such a place; so was he.

The vision, the realization did not unfold, but came through like some unimaginable hyperideogram which conveyed not: a word, a unit of meaning, but entire developed monographs. Then, to untangle it and spread it out linearly, he had to *think*. Pass.

Thelledy was the subject. Galitzyn was the subject. In his inner vision, it moved internally, rotated, and assembled itself, the known, into an abstract structure in five dimensions which, could it be projected coherently onto the Plane, would look something like an ideogram manifested in repeating detail. All Demsing did was to nudge it into an "assembly" state, and release, and of itself, it fell into a completed state, and then he could retreat back into *thinking* to untangle it within the plodding pace of Linear Time.

Item: Thelledy was a long-term mole who had been trained very well somewhere else on Teragon and planted in this group for long-term goals.

Item: Thelledy was of near certainty a *Kobith* of the Wa'an Assassins, and now he saw the difference between Thelledy and the girl whom the Carrionflower had caught. Of virtual certainty was the fact that she had checked the passenger list of the *Vitus Bering*, looking for someone specific, and those who might have deduced that were conveniently lost not long after.

Item: There was a long-term operation, partly offworld, maybe its major part offworld, targeted on him, Demsing, and contracted through the best-run operation on the planet.

Item: Pitalny Vollbrecht was certainly on Teragon, now. And where was the best possible place to hide an offworlder? In the one place where he didn't have to *do* anything: the Group Mind. He could be trained offworld in the basics and, once in place, updated by the worldwide Wa'an network. He would be impressive, and accurate. And

Galitzyn had appeared after the *Bering* had come. This had other ramifications which were alarming indeed.

Item: There would be no revenge for the girl who had been caught by the Carrionflower in Meroe, not within an operation of this scale. She had been expendable—and there was a strong possibility that she had been sent to fail, as some sort of punishment.

Item: The worst thing about answers was that they posed more questions, world without end. What was it he had or used that made him an object of an elaborate plot? He reviewed the chain of circumstances, and found it still standing. He was neither jumping at shadows nor reading into things. The surveillance of the girl in Meroe was fact, Vollbrecht was fact, and the connection of Wa'an to Thelledy to Galtizyn was fact, and all of the latter part could be easily verified by tests he could perform without their being aware of it. Subtle and some trouble, yes, but worth it, now, because he could not move further without determining what he faced, and then performing the proper maneuver to neutralize it. But that was a separate operation, and one of his limits seemed to be that it was, itself, a demanding process which cost a lot in terms of energy.

5

We tend to reach only for those things whose ends may be seen clearly, and then wonder why their promise evaporates even as we grasp them most tightly. To get close to an answer is to suggest that we do not see clearly, no matter what we say. But closer still is the realization that the real things that matter, that ultimately define our lives, what we are and who we are, are invariably and precisely those things whose ends we cannot see, or will not see.

H. C., Atropine Extracts

The Archive, or Mind, of an organization was a valuable quantity and protected at all times, from himself or herself, or others, as required. In the case of Klippisch's small organization, this duty was exchanged between Dossifey and Thelledy, when Galitzyn was not working directly with Klippisch herself. Dossifey took most of the shifts, mainly because he had been with the organization longest. Thelledy took fewer, because she had been with them a lesser time, but it was a measure of the trust that Klippisch held her in that she got them at all, and she had earned that trust by a demonstrated unswerving loyalty to the things Klippisch directed, a quality she held to be rare in "these degenerate times."

The watch duties were not demanding; keep the Mind safe, and make sure he got rest. Thelledy always did this by moving the location around in a random manner and keeping Galitzyn in places only she seemed to know, and frequently contacting Klippisch or whoever was acting with her at that time.

It also provided an opportunity for Thelledy to make contact with Galitzyn. She had chosen this place with care, even more than her usual standard, which was always high by the standards of Teragon: a small, bare apartment which at some time in the past had been added on after the fashion of the planet to a large exhalor, an air shaft connecting with the deep interior levels. Here, the oxygen level was noticeably high and the temperature was more comfortable than the Teragon norm. It also had a good view on all sides and was difficult to approach, concealed.

Galitzyn had, in his own past, thought himself a fairly competent field operative. He was alert, he noticed things many others, themselves considered proficient, missed. Here, in this place, he sometimes doubted the wisdom of coming here. This district, Desimetre, was widely considered to be relatively safe for offworlders, according to Teragon practices, but it had required every resource he possessed to maintain his cover here, and from what he had heard, he doubted seriously if he could survive more than a few standard days anywhere else on this planet.

He thought of it as The Feral Planet, where humans had, in the course of time, turned into something quite unimaginable. The natives here seemed to be immune to all the accepted forms of manipulation practiced elsewhere, and had taken on values which were difficult to describe, if at all. Definitions had a way of dissolving here. And despite the fact that the surface was completely covered with what might be called a vast and poorly organized city, it was, to all evidence, severely under-populated. The humans who lived there seemed like scattered survivors inhabiting ruins built to house a population much higher.

Thelledy always raised these questions. On the surface, she seemed to be a young woman, more than normally pleasant in appearance, with an oval, soft face, loose thick, black hair which was cut short, and a sturdy, muscular figure. But other things about her terrified him. She appeared to have no possessions whatsoever and formed no attachments he was aware of. He had no idea where she lived, if that was the word for what she did on her own time. And she moved in Time with an awareness he could barely imagine. And by her own estimation, she rated herself "above average, but not completely excellent." Galitzyn often found himself wishing he would never meet someone she looked up to.

She had such an estimation of Demsing. As she had put it to him once, "Demsing at full awareness cannot be countered by any one operative I know of, which is why he keeps himself as secretive as he does; if he were to become widely known, he would cease to have value, because of that. We check ourselves and each other, and simply put, one-on-one, he can't be covered."

"Then your group would not hire him, having formed that estimation?"

"No. We wouldn't anyway, for other reasons, but even if we did outside contracting, we wouldn't hire him. He is totally independent."

"How many people know that, here?"

"We know it. Now you do. We won't sell that to anybody, and you can't, so he's safe."

"Why wouldn't you sell that information?"

"He voluntarily does not oppose our goals directly, and does not contest with us in any area."

That had sounded curious, but no more so than the usual responses he got, here.

Galitzyn knew very little about Thelledy; she was his contact here, and an apparently junior member of an organization which was composed predominantly of women, deadly women. He himself had not established the working relationship, so he had no idea how it had been arranged, or who they were. They were being paid to track Demsing, and they would lose him often, and they were accounted the best of the groups that operated planetwide.

From her side, all she knew was that offworlders wanted Demsing tracked, and if possible, brought to an area where they could observe him directly. She never allowed her contempt to show openly, but Galitzyn could read it there, all the same.

According to the chronometers which everyone wore, it was standard night. Outside, through the single window, he could see Primary moving across the dark sky, casting razor shadows that looked sharp enough to cut the careless.

Thelledy slipped into the room with a graceful minimum of motion that for a moment beguiled him. She said, without preliminaries, "Well, he's here, now. What are you going to do with him?"

"What's he doing currently?"

"Ostensibly training the kids he's been given. I spotted him a girl, and he took the bait."

"That's not usual for him, is it?"

"Not usual at all. We estimate it doesn't make any difference to him, however, so don't expect any leverage. He does that every so often."

"What? Picks up a girl?"

Thelledy favored Galitzyn with a glance one might see in a housekeeper looking at a roach. "No. He forms relationships, with people who have no apparent value, and trains them. Somehow he can see a value in them others can't; at any rate, he manages to turn them into extraordinary people. Useless to us, I might add. This girl, Chalmour, I rated as subnormal and bumbling, not really trainable even for this group, so for me, she was a throwaway. He scooped her up like he'd found gold. We know from past observation that he's seen something valuable in her and will bring it out. What it is we can't determine. Why don't you ask him?"

For some reason, this frightened Galitzyn more

than anything she could have said, and he knew she knew it.

"The report I'm sending back at next contact will suggest that there may not be a way to contact him for what we have in mind. We thought putting an operator in place here might clarify this problem, which we have had for some time, but I don't see any way clear to make contact without a level of hazard we can't risk."

"What do you people want him for? I mean, he's certainly one of the best, but if you can hire us, you can pay for what you want, and with a good, tight operation, surely a combination could be found that could do it."

"That's the problem. He's operating, the best we can determine, at about 10 percent of capacity. Teragon isn't even a challenge to him. He acts as if he doesn't know what he can do. So we would have to tell him that, and that's the dangerous part."

"Your people rate him as dangerous?"

She had asked this before, but continued to ask it from time to time, as if she did not believe his answers.

"More dangerous than you can imagine, if he's contacted wrong."

"Well, the only way we deal with him is, by and large, with candor. We have found out that you can't hide much from him, once he gets on the scent. That was how we got him here, you know, and that was iffy. And by the way, when do you people compensate us for the loss of Asztali?"

Galitzyn bridled a little, "I thought that was

covered from your end. She was supposed to fail, wasn't she?"

"You know the contract as well as I do: you pay for losses. At no time were we to engage him openly. Nor would we, and that's from the top. They rate him even higher than I do. She was to fail, that is true, but the method was more drastic than required. She was not supposed to fall into a Carrion-flower, and normally wouldn't have. We are investigating why that happened."

"You don't know?"

Thelledy left it unanswered. After a time, Galitzyn said, "I'll see to it. Goes out next report. The usual rates?"

"The usual."

"Do you know where he is at this moment? I saw that he left for a while."

"Went home with Chalmour, over in the Palterie somewhere. Now *that's* unusual, I can tell you that. Girls, yes. Boys, even, occasionally. But taking them home? Definitely out of character!"

"What do you have on this Chalmour?"

"To us, she's ordinary." She shrugged, as if the girl weren't worth discussing.

"Why would he go to her parents' home with her?"

"We can't predict his actions. He must have reasons even more opaque. I can think of several possibilities, some of which are relatively innocent ... some aren't." Again, she shrugged. "You see, we know from his actions we've tracked that whatever he does with her won't affect us."

"Why is that?"

"Because he doesn't build organizations. He destroys them."

Galitzyn seemed to shrink. He said, softly, "We know that."

Demsing had done something slightly more intricate than Thelledy's report might have it; he had, it was true, "gone home with Chalmour." But that wasn't all of it. What he actually had done was take his entire crew of apprentices off on an extended field trip into the apparently boundless suburbs of The Palterie, where they supported themselves by doing a wide range of small tasks, some of which were simple and ordinary odd jobs by any planet's estimation, and some of which were beginner's exercises in the kind of subtle sophistication Demsing preferred. All of the apprentices enjoyed this and performed at their best.

What he had learned from Chalmour had motivated him to follow this course. She was the youngest member of what had been a large family for Teragon, and her parents still had the room to house them all, provided they could contribute to the ongoing operations of the house. Klippisch knew about it and approved.

More importantly, Chalmour's parents approved. They had managed to place six children without failure, none of them expert but all competent survivors, and they had thought Chalmour a little slow, and were delighted with Demsing, despite the apparent age difference between himself and the girl. True, he was an unknown stranger, and bore the marks of a fearsome competence, but he treated her well, and took time with her. Their relationship was obviously still new, but already they could see changes in her which seemed well, for her future. She still retained her flighty sense of humor, but moved about the things she did with a new sense of precision and confidence, and if Demsing gave her this out of a sense of potential he saw in her, that was all to the good. That was why they had sent her to Klippisch in the first place.

While the apprentices were all out on one of Demsing's exercises, Demsing brought this subject and others out in the open with the girl's parents, Elsonek and Lelkempre.

Elsonek began, "We have to make excuses in this day and this place for feelings of overprotection."

"Don't apologize; far too many send them out without a word of encouragement."

Lelkempre added, "Too often, you have to look another way ..."

Demsing said, "We do have a lot of this here; I have often wondered about that. Undoubtedly that attitude certainly produces survivors, but its cost is high in the ... development of things that sometimes lie hidden."

Elsonek asked, "Then you see something special in Chalmour, something you can enhance?"

"Not really. She is mostly what she seems. The difference in her is that she is open enough to allow me to bring it out of her, what seems to lie quietly hidden in most of us. From that standpoint, she is very special, but not in any abstract sense, but in the particular case of her and me."

"Why should you do this thing?"

Demsing understood the question. Elsonek and Lelkempre were astute enough to recognize part of what Demsing was within the context of Teragon—a confident and powerful self-supported individual who operated without outside backing. He worked for himself. And so why should such a person, who could obviously have the symbols of competence with little effort, choose a girl like Chalmour, who was pleasant enough, but who did not seem to be remarkable in any way?

He answered, "There are those who would see this as an indulgence; after all, most people indulge if they can. This is not the case. There is something real there, rare enough for me to feel I should follow it. She is good for me, and apparently I do the same for her. I am not a justifier, nor a signifier, one to prevent unique events because of sets of abstract principles. Too long I have lived for myself."

"Then there is no concealed purpose in this."

"If there is anything concealed, it is what Chalmour can become after I have taught her to bring it out and protect herself while she's doing it."

Lelkempre exclaimed, "You don't know what you're going to get!"

"Exactly that!"

Elsonek suggested, "You might get something you wouldn't like so much."

"To endure difference is to grow; most people are fixated children because once they obtain power, they strive to make everything in their own image."

"Then your intent is long range. That would include, of necessity, children."

"In the usual case. I, however, do not reproduce. I do not know the reason. Nothing appears to malfunction. There are more than enough strays on Teragon—we can make do adequately with those." As Demsing said that, he felt an odd and immensely strong sense of déjà vu, as if either the words, or the image underlying them, were a life he'd lived before. It was so strong it forced him off the track of the present, in this house, now, and he had to exert considerable effort to return to it. The sensation of recapitulating something within himself was overpowering, but he could not identify it, and as he thought to search for it in memory, it faded and vanished even as he reached for it. "Fertile, ah, that is correct: I am sterile."

"You have spoken with her about these things?"

"Yes."

"Why would you bring them to us? Chalmour is, after all, on her own in these things and has been for some time."

"I cannot explain further than it seemed the proper thing to do. I normally do not question such suggestions of perception. Chalmour is as unique to me as I am to her, and something out of the ordinary practice seemed . . . well, correct. That was another unique event in itself, our conversation on this, but it echoes the uniqueness of the relationship in a resonant manner. The two reinforce each other. You might say legitimize."

Elsonek laughed, "Nothing is legitimate on Teragon!"

"Perhaps it should be, and perhaps this might be the place to start."

Elsonek glanced at Lelkempre. He said, "Some sort of response seems to be necessary at this point . . . I will permit it." Lelkempre nodded her agreement. "I do ask that you train her properly before you turn her loose; she is a bit scatterbrained."

Demsing nodded in return, as if the ritual whose outlines he could only guess had been fulfilled. "If such comes to be, she may leave of her own will. I, however, have no such intent."

Lelkempre said, "Nor does she. She has spoken with us about this. And so I tell you that same I told her: you have opened up something rare and valuable—something people search for all their lives and do not find. But beware its power, too. It is dangerous. We all know that instinctively."

"I would like to create a world in which such dangers, as you call them, were not dangers, but were seen for what they really were, prized gifts."

Elsonek turned sharply at this and said, "And what about the rest?"

"There are corrosive evils we have learned to ignore, and whose consequences we accept as if they were natural, if unhappy, accidents. These elements and the consequential world they form as they unfold are generated by an ancient fear which I should like to remove."

Elsonek said, "Most do not ask such questions."

Demsing responded, "They do not ask because they fear the potential of the answers; as if one could always ask, 'could I live independently, on my own?' But they almost never ask it out of the fear of possible negative. More, they build a conceptual universe in which such questions cannot even be framed, and one more step, too, that of building a logical system within whose bounds clear evidence is arrayed into distorted patterns called straight. There is a lot of learning and a lot of Time behind such habits, and it is neither easy nor casual to unstructure such artifacts."

"I might agree that such an artifact exists, but what was the reason for its construction?"

"The best I can tell you now is that it appears that it exists to prevent perception of, and implementation thereof, the obvious, to favor specific attitudes of those who found they could control groups by obstructing that flow."

Elsonek looked away. "You have said a lot."

"I have said more than I intended, and more than I have dared say to anyone before. It is difficult to frame it in speech which has been deliberately designed to blur and obscure it. This did not originate here on Teragon, but has deep roots in Time. It was brought here, and found a fertile soil which allows it to express itself here with particular clarity. But if that amplification makes it, the idea, particularly powerful over us, it also makes it particularly perceptible, and hence, vulnerable."

"That is a heavy load for, as you say, an ordinary girl."

"It is no load at all, and its resolution is within the grasp of all of us; only the way to say it, so to speak, is hard."

Lelkempre said, "Make enough money to leave,

and buy your way offplanet, to a better world, the two of you."

"I could do so, but I know the answer is here, strange as that sounds."

Demsing set the apprentices on some more exercises, with Chalmour set up as a loose control, and then left them behind while he made a quick trip back to Desimetre, under the tightest level of covered movement he could manage. Should anyone have been following him or keeping him under surveillance, they would have seen him do simple, ordinary things, and fade from view, and then vanish.

Faren Kiricky lived in a modest, but comfortable house in the part of Desimetre closest to Gueldres, a plain masonry structure of one main room and two smaller ones added on the sides, topped with the low dome characteristic of the houses of Desimetre. There was a wall around the front part, enclosing a small patio on which a Suntracker plant was displayed in a large pot.

The Suntracker was another of the odd plants found on Teragon whose origin could not be explained. Growing from a thick, sturdy trunk, it expanded its form in a series of random and assymetric tiers of flat structures assumed to be leaves, which moved constantly so as to maintain a constant angle on Primary. Here its resemblance to a plant ended, for the trunk and branches were a bright metallic blue, reticulated and scaled like the hide of some ophidian creature, and the "leaves" were delicate, fleshy structures colored in iridescent patterns of changing colors. During the short "day" of Teragon, the leaves tracked the course of Primary with unerring accuracy, and during the night, it reset itself to that point on its horizon where Primary would reappear.

The Suntracker was a luxury, because it required considerable care to maintain it in its best condition, and the treatment suggested an origin whose environmental conditions were odd in the extreme. It required watering with a precise solution of 1 percent hydrogen peroxide, and trace amounts of a peculiar compound, arsenous selenide applied at rare intervels. After such treatment, the plant would give off a faint odor of mustard, which had been found to be infinitesimal amounts of arsine gas.

Demsing found Faren at home, as it were, giving the Suntracker one of its periodic treatments. He let himself in the gate, just as he had when he had lived there. She did not seem surprised to see him, but stood and held out her hands to him, which he took.

Demsing saw that Faren had aged, as he had expected, but Time had been surprisingly kind to her. She was still trim of figure, active and precise in her movements, although her hair had turned white and her face was thinner and traced by a fine network of lines.

He said, "You look well; you always do."

"Nonsense. I am falling apart. It is all I can do now to crawl out of bed; but you look fit. Have you been busy?"

"Well enough. I have not been bored, that's a fact."

"Klippisch had them tell me you were about."

"Yes. I wanted to wait awhile before I came to see you; it seemed the right way to do it."

Faren did not question this. Demsing had always seemed to move according to some subtle internal timer, and it had always seemed to work out best to let things happen according to it. She said, "Are you living with anyone?"

"A girl, from here now, but originally from the Palterie."

"Good, I approve. It is not good to live alone."

"I'm looking for a way to put some permanence in it."

"That would also be to the good. Doubtless you'll have to change your ways."

"That's what I'm looking for. Difficult to find, though."

"I quite understand, now. At first I didn't, here, but. . . . There is a way, if you can find it. You will, eventually."

"Yes."

"Have you time to come in?"

"Yes. I had wanted to ask you some things."

"Come in, then." Faren finished the few remaining tasks with the Suntracker, and motioned Demsing to follow her into the house. The large part, under the main dome, contained a few simple things, much as he remembered it: a narrow bed on one side, a table and two chairs on the other. It also had a window facing the patio, arched across the top, framing the view of the Suntracker. The smaller sections contained a kitchen and a bathroom, respectively. The floor was covered by a woven rug of geometric patterns. On one wall was a contrastgraph image of Dorje, a severe black and white representation which expressed an image of a face solely by the highlights of it, in themselves random patterns of no specific shape which the mind assembled into a face. On the other was a similar contrastgraph of himself as a young boy. By the door was another, depicting the face of a young woman which, by its full and rounded contours, seemed to suggest a full-figured body. All was as it had always been, including the contrastgraphs. Demsing had never known who the woman was. He had always been told, "It was someone we wanted to remember," and that had been all there was to it. He had not followed it out; Teragon, he had learned at an early age, did not permit the luxury of nostalgia or reminiscences.

The house was cool and quiet, with an imperceptible scent of familiar things used and kept up for a long time. How long?

Faren prepared them a simple meal of noodles, an oil or sauce which was a disturbing carmine color but which had a bland and inoffensive taste, some greens, and a bowl of chickpeas, served with a honey-colored near-beer. During the meal, they did not talk, but savored the rarity of the time and the silence. He remembered it well: it always had been a quiet house, a refuge, and she had kept it that way.

Finishing, Faren ventured, "How does it seem?"

"Like always. Things never change here. That is difficult to do."

"I would let it change, or more away, sometimes, but then I don't. We have only one life—why live it in an uproar? I moved around a lot as a girl, and Dorje had also. When we came here, it wasn't at all like we expected, and so we worked to make this place something . . . special." It was, to Demsing, the simple statement of someone who had learned to live within her limits without resentment or envy, and he admired Faren for attaining it, and expressing it thus as well.

He thought a moment, and then said, "You could have gone back to space. For that matter, you could have stayed there."

She shrugged. "Possibly."

Demsing began, "I have a problem, which I haven't taken to anyone else, and I am uncertain how to approach it."

"Is it the same as you had before? The visions of places you'd never been?"

"Yes, that. Only now there are more of them, more often, than there used to be, and they are clearer. To one, they feel like memories."

Faren busied herself in the kitchen with the dishes and avoided Demsing's eyes. It was a problem she had, within her limits, tried to ignore in the hope that it would go away. But of course, it hadn't. Demsing was Nazarine, and she knew him as both, and by implication, all the other lives Nazarine had told her she had been, as the Morphodite: Nazarine Alea, Phaedrus, Damistofia Azart, Rael, Jedily Tulilly. Nazarine was the face in the third contrastgraph.

The Morphodite had the ability to *change*, to undergo a terrifying metamorphosis into another person, of different gender and about twenty years lower age, sometimes more, sometimes less. Nazarine had been her friend, but she had herself seen Nazarine's powers of perception work, and also her power to *change* ... the last time, the change had produced an infant with premature characteristics, which she and Dorje Ngellathy had taken and accepted responsibility for.

Faren did not entirely understand the process, which seemed to generate its own peculiar rules as it went, rules which seemed, as anything unknown, to be arbitrary and capricious. But one thing which was constant seemed to be the retention of memory. There was a slippage from one persona to another, as if the process of change did not carry over the entire memory, but edited it down into some condensed form. It had been Nazarine's opinion that having to pass through infancy would limit severely the memory of the past and that the resultant persona would forget or never remember being The Morphodite, live out a normal life, and vanish from the stage.

It had been her hope, too. But it had not been long before the child, Demsing, had begun to display unusual abilities, and to have "visions," as he had put it. She and Dorje, while Dorje had lived, had neither suppressed such things in the growing boy, nor had they encouraged them. They had cautioned him about revealing his unusual abilities and perceptions to anyone, and so he had grown up with it.

As Demsing had matured, the unknown abilities had not lessened, but instead had grown, and had enabled him to become, with envied ease, an adept and ruthless operative in the endless personal conflict which passed for society on Teragon. Demsing drew on the capabilities of The Morphodite without knowing their source. In a sense, then, Demsing was innocent of the full extent of his powers, and more dangerously, innocent entirely of the uses to which such powers could be put.

Faren knew some of it from Nazarine, but she suspected she was only a witness of a part of it, and at that, a part Nazarine had held back. And now the problem had not gone away, indeed, but had come back, rather more oppressive than before. It was, after all, a question of how Demsing realized what he could do, that would determine how he used it, or if he used it.

She and Dorje had worked on that assumption, and tried to build a strong and secure character in Demsing. And to their credit, a considerable part of it had taken; Demsing had no traces of sadism, cruelty, perversity, or bizarre urges, and did not, to her knowledge, exploit others because of their weaknesses, as many did. But the other side of the Demsing coin was that he represented a peak in the type of ideal citizen of Teragon, competent and ruthless where such behavior was called for. Demsing, in short, had turned out well, according to the ideals, if one could call them that, of Teragon. But no one could foresee what he was capable of, if he regained his full powers and memory of his pasts.

She said, "Medicine here has remained rudimentary, simple survival medicine, almost like combat medicine. So they never developed much in psychiatrics. I don't even know whom we could ask to help you with that. In fact, there may not be anyone on Teragon who could. How much of a problem is it?"

She watched him closely. Demsing had always been something of a mystery to her. He was of average height, but something about his movements seemed to make him appear shorter, and similarly, although he had a slight build, he seemed stocky. His face bore virtually no distinguishing marks, but people always remembered him as seeming "hard" and "determined." Perhaps. She did not know the girl he had met, and she wondered what *she* saw in that face.

Demsing put his hands behind his head and leaned back. "I can handle it if I have to. I just thought you might have heard something, somebody who worked with these things. I have looked along such lines as I can, and I can't find anyone, nor can I find anyone with this condition. Do you have any idea why this might be?"

"No. We saw it in you at an early age and had no explanation for it. It never seemed like a sickness, just something extra we never could explain. And conditions here, then, were the same as now. We had no experts to turn to."

"In Pontossaget District, there's a place where they keep lunatics; I even looked into their visions, or what they would reveal of them, and there's no comparison. But I think I may be on the verge of solving part of it."

"You are?"

"Yes. It's just a suspicion right now, but . . . this is really hard to explain. But basically, I have had a suspicion for some time that I can build these fragments back into something like their original shape. I can't explain how it works, because there simply aren't words for it. Up to now, one thing or another has prevented it, but . . . It takes time, you understand, and that I've had little of, and few enough to cover me while I experiment with it. I don't question now that the fragments are real. I've tested some of them, and they meet every validity test, which dreams and hallucinations do not."

Faren said, carefully, "I would be frightened to experiment with my own mind, if that is what you're doing."

Demsing looked blandly at her across the room. "It's not, if you anchor the reference system in reality, the outside, and everybody's always said I was good at reality."

"Yes, that's true. Still . . ."

"Well, I'd like to get to the bottom of it, you know. I think it's dangerous to me to be walking around with something in my head whose nature I don't know. After all, it could be something more strange than we could imagine—it could be some kind of projection from another person. I want to isolate all the alternative explanations."

"I don't know what to say, except that you must be careful, and remember who you are at all times."

"Yes! Odd that you said it that way: that's just what it feels like: remembering who I am."

6

Certainly, we perceivers, recorders, revealers of phenomena need most earnestly to learn to stalk and attack live prey—by that I mean current, contemporary superstitions, shibboleths, and fetishes which arise of our own world now, and not waste our time and that of our audience by beating, however vigorously, the dead horses of a past generation.

H. C., Atropine

Demsing collected the four apprentices and returned to Desimetre, and set up a local routine again. Klippisch was so pleased with the changes she could see for herself that she put Demsing on the duty of guarding Galitzyn, relieving Dossifey of some of the work.

Although he had not influenced this action, he could see the value of it instantly, and made the most of it on the first shift he took.

He started by rambling on at some length about the progress he had made with the four apprentices he'd been given, and with special emphasis on Chalmour.

Galitzyn rose to the bait like a novice of less skill than the apprentices, waiting until the conversation in the safe house hit a soft spot, and asked, "You've taken an interest in Chalmour."

Demsing did not look at Galitzyn, fearing the leer of triumph on his face would be obvious even to this offworlder. "Well, in fact it did work out that way."

"Are you looking further than tomorrow?"

He answered, shyly, as if wishing to conceal it, "We have talked about it. You know how these things go; one never knows, that's all. One day . . . there you are. You understand things you missed when you didn't know they were lacking before. Would, do you think, Klippisch be interested in making this more permanent?"

"Possibly. More than that, actually. She is well pleased with you."

"Um. I'll bring it up with her in a bit. I've got something else to work on, in the meantime—a little private project, so to speak, Research, you might call it."

Galitzyn looked oddly at Demsing. "What sort of 'research'?"

"A thing I'd like to settle before I make hard commitments involving others. Basically, what I need for this part of it is to have a long conversation with a specialist in psychiatric healing . . . there doesn't seem to be such a person in easy reach."

Demsing could hear the confusion in Galitzyn's voice. "There's always Pontossaget."

"They don't know anything. They just lock them up."

Galitzyn was silent a long time, weighing something. Finally he offered, "There's supposed to be a certain lady down in the lower levels, Tudomany by name, who has a varying success in that area. Be advised I personally rate her as something between a witch and a faith healer, but one always hears things."

"Tudomany . . . I've heard that name."

"Way down. Near the Lysine section, below Gueldras."*

"I thought I heard she was old. Does this Tudomany still live?"

"Far as I know. She tells fortunes too."

Demsing allowed a low laugh to slide around and sang, off key, "She made a fortune sellin' voodoo, and interpret the dream!"**

"You'll never make a singer! Where did you hear *that*?"

"Don't know. Some song I heard once, I guess. Well, that will work really well—I can combine a field trip with that."

"Chalmour. . . ?"

"Yes. She's ready for that phase."

"What do you plan to do with her?"

---

*Food on Teragon was manufactured, not grown. Some was cultured in hydroponic vats underground, other components were synthesized, either directly (chemically) or else as the product of fermentation vats. Certain compounds were easily made, others were more difficult. Some were rare and valuable. Lysine, an amino acid, was one of them.
** "Marie Laveau, Part I," Oscar "Papa" Celestin.

"Teach her. She trusts me." And that was the truth.

If Galitzyn had based his estimates of the under-population of Teragon on what he had seen on the surface, underground the discrepancy was even more marked. Groups and individuals who could not cope with the surface often went underground, if for no other reason than there was more room, indeed, so it seemed, endless amounts of it. The problem for them all was that the underground was an endless labyrinth with many dead ends, closed passages, and areas which were being rebuilt to support some new surface artifact.

And if it had been Demsing's aim to stir the net watching him into a series of actions which would bring them into a more open and a vulnerable position, he could not have selected a better tale, nor one to tell it to. He had reasoned that if whoever Galitzyn represented had had a watch on him for as long as he thought they had, the report of two apparently irrational breaks with the past pattern might move them to move unwisely. The one was Chalmour, and what made it work with particular validity was the fact that it was true. The second part was more subtle, an attempt to see if he could find out what they really wanted of him.

He also had little doubt who would actually cover his trip underground: Thelledy or one of her associates from nearby. As to recognizing who the shadow might be, he didn't worry about that at all. Long ago he had developed the habit of learning what they were before he unraveled who they were, picking up fragments from the background and putting them together, knowing that the more the operator relied on an external system of training and discipline, the more obvious they became.

He stopped by the safe house and picked up Chalmour. As they set out into the twilight day of Teragon, she asked, "Aren't we going to take any food packs with us, any weapons?"

"No, and no. If they are covering us to the degree I think they are, they would see that immediately as preparations for a long trip, or perhaps a siege somewhere. Preparations for a siege invites besiegers. As for the weapons . . . we have what we can easily conceal on us. You brought yours?"

"Yes. All the ones I can handle easily, not the new ones I don't do so well on yet."

"Good." He reached to her and touched her face, and she moved close beside him, brushing her shoulder against his and looking up at him expectantly. It was at these moments that Demsing felt most tempted to abandon the whole thing, vanish and elude them somehow, and just run away. Today she was wearing her favorite clothing, loose pants, a sweater with a hood, soft low boots all faded with age into an indescribable gray-tan color that would blend well underground. And it was moments like these when it was most difficult to perceive her. Demsing was well aware of the classical lover's problem, of not being able to form a clear image of your lover's face in one's mind, except with great effort; he knew it went further than that, to all the senses. You never identified the lover with any particular scent, either, or taste. She tasted like pure water, and smelled like pure air. He believed that this sensory blindless had a purpose—to establish a deeper perception which almost entirely ignored the body and any specific feature of it. If the deeper perception was there, the body would become the perfect object of desire, knowing that the real desire was something much deeper. They had walked into that and had been caught in it before either one of them had realized what was happening.

She was slender and wiry, more angular and boyish than most girls, but she moved with a smooth grace and a fluidity which no male could hope to match. Her face was the most arresting thing about her, although Demsing knew very well that any face was not beautiful in itself, but in what it expressed and what the expectations of the seer were. An interaction. Chalmour's face was delicate toward the chin, and given an interesting accent by a longish nose which lay close to the planes of her face and had been given an additional emphasis by having been broken in a fall. Her eyes were deepset and dark-brown, her mouth thin and concise. It was a wry and agile face that expressed emotions well.

At first they walked along openly, almost idly strolling, looking into passing shops and commenting on certain buildings of Desimetre which had an odd or erratic air about them. This part of the City was relatively well-lit, with some overheads, lights and beacons on many of the buildings, and watchlights at curbs and low walls. The effect was pleasant, relaxed, and an impression of security. Here, as elsewhere on Teragon, the buildings were low, one, two or three stories, made of the inevitable *kamen* masonry, with rounded corners and many low domes. Demsing had once seen a travel poster of Old Earth, depicting a Greek island in the Aegean sea, and that was what Desimetre most closely resembled, except that it was always illuminated in its day by a light that resembled extremely strong moonlight more than the "sunlight" of a more normal world.

Primary was rising ahead of them in the northwest behind Gueldres, a hot, cream-colored or pearly spot with a visible disk which moved as one watched it, a BB shot at arm's-length, while around them the magic sharp shadows moved and flowed along the streets.* Demsing knew that he had probably instigated something drastic, possibly final, but despite that, or because of it, he felt a spring come into his step.

Even at the close orbital radius of 17 million miles, Primary, although possessing one solar mass, was in fact a body only 8200 miles in diameter and at that distance, it did not appear to be a very large object; it did not appear to be a *sun* at all, but an intensely bright star which displayed a small disk. It may be added that with an F spectrum from the light-emitting surface, it was also cool for such objects, implying greater age than the far more common A-spectrum white dwarfs. It may also be added here that the region about the Primary/Teragon System was thin in gases and dust and that there were no other orbiting bodies in the system, so that Primary was exceptionally stable and did not exhibit detectable fluctuations. No companion body to this system, i.e., another star, gravitationally bound, has ever been discovered.

Chalmour said, "We should begin evading; even I can feel the pressure."

"You notice it?"

"Yes. It is clear sometimes, sometimes fading out, but always there. What did you tell them?"

Demsing shrugged and grinned at her. "The Truth."

"Well, you know how dangerous *that* is."

"Sometimes you have to risk that, that way, to get the kind of reaction you want. I want to draw them out into the open a little, so they can make a mistake."

"You have actually told me very little about this."

"I don't know very much. Somebody's following me, but they don't seem to want to close for action, and they hold back from coming closer. I tried to figure out what they want from me, but I don't have enough data . . . yet."

"The way they expose themselves will give you that?"

"It could. It may. You learn to see patterns of organization, rhythms, it's like that, nothing more."

"You make it sound simple. I rather have a time trying even the simple tricks you tried to show me."

"You do mine better than you do Thelledy's . . ."

"Oh, *those*, ha ha!" She pressed his arm quickly. "I think I do well enough for me on my own, thank you."

"Well, as far as evading them, now is not the time. We want them to see beyond a shadow of a doubt where we're going. That will confuse them even more, because they expect me to deceive them."

"Have you an option for no reaction from them?"

"Yes. Vanish."

"You will vanish with me?"

"Without a doubt."

"Then we might not ever come back from this walk?"

"That's right. Might never come back. But that's nothing different from living every day here. Most people, even here, fear that profoundly and though they may preach it, they don't practice it by a long shot. When every moment might be your last, you live out each one to its full potential. And of course you have to be ready to move instantly and take off across the world to a district you've never seen, and not only survive, but prosper."

Chalmour said nothing for a long time. Finally she said, "That's like that old nonsense joke about the boy and girl walking underground in this endless tunnel, and she says, 'Olvaso, where are we going?' and he replies, 'Just keep walking.' But before you tell me to keep walking, what I want to know is how you could evade them there?"

"I know they're looking, now. That makes a difference. Before, I didn't know."

By now, they had come a good distance west along one of the streets of Desimetre which followed an imaginary contour and mostly kept to an equivalent elevation. Ahead, however, all ways dipped slightly and went down, to the left into Ctameron with its squat sleek towers, and right, to the district of Gueldres, which had an old-time air of respectability and probity to it, an atmosphere of business affairs of long tradition carried on at a slow and relaxed pace designed to bring out and enhance every nuance, simply for style.

Entering Gueldres, crossing a line that was no less definitive for all that it was, in the most obvious sense, invisible, Demsing and Chalmour continued along the street, which now seemed deeper between the buildings, although the buildings were not especially higher, nor the street deeper. The effect seemed to be a reflection of nothing more substantial than a subtle change of style, certain lines emphasized while others were concealed, so that the street *seemed* narrower.

There were also many more gratings covering lower passages, and there was less an illusion of being on a hard surface. Demsing went along these ways openly and directly, but not hurriedly, and seemed to know exactly where he was going. And when a kiosk indicated the opening to a set of steep metal stairs leading downwards, they entered without pausing and followed the stairs down into the lower parts of Gueldres.

The stairs, which were broad enough for six abreast, continued downwards in sections interrupted by a landing in the middle, doubling back at each level they passed. At first, on the upper levels, there were rather more people about their affairs than in the streets of the surface, which was true of Gueldres, that it was developed vertically more than horizontally. But even lower, the numbers rapidly dropped off and by the time they were ten levels down, there were hardly any people at all. Their steps on the metal rang into eerie echoes.

Here, there were few shops, if any. Occasionally they saw open areas where pumping operations were carried out, mostly by automatic machinery with a mechanic on duty, or else offices, or, more rarely, large open areas where it seemed some sort of chemical refining operations were being carried out.

The nature of the corridors changed as well; on the upper levels, the corridors were similar to the street in width and seemed to follow the general patterns of the streets, only they did not extend very far in any straight direction. But lower, this sense of replicating patterns faded and the corridors narrowed until the cross section became square, and the side walls began to take on an unmistakable look of solidity. At each landing, what seemed to be the main corridor might lead off in any direction. Some seemed to end at the landings and go off a short distance before turning a corner, or appearing to end.

Chalmour said, quietly, just slightly above a whisper, "I can't say I like this very much."

Demsing agreed mildly. "True. You can't move around as well, here. Of course, it also limits how well followers can work, too."

"I picked up some of them, topside."

"You did better than I expected; I could see you make them. But you only saw a third or so."

"How do they commmunicate?"

"Hand signs or body gestures. In a good team that has trained together, such methods actually are faster, within a certain area, than electronics, because there's no interpretation step going through a machine. Let's get off, here."

"And you don't see them carrying equipment."

"No. They have none. Down here, of course, they'll have to rely more on machine transmission systems, sampling, and reports into some central point. We won't see so many people, but the percentage of watchers will actually go up. There will be places we pass where all of the people we see are watchers, or certainly, no less than eight out of every ten."

"What's down here?"

"More stations, plant operations, pumps, generators, that kind of thing. There are people. I've not ever been so far down I saw none at all. And of course you get some more predatory types down here, who try to live on the leavings that filter down from above. They are normally extremely cautious and one has little to fear, but it is wise to remain alert."

The landing at this level seemed to be in a kind of dead end, but the walls around them had metal doors which seemed to have no locks. One way, the corridor narrowed to a hallway and turned, but there were slot lights alternating along the floor and ceiling lines, so there was plenty of light, and, so it seemed, a blurred muttering which seemed to indicate people and machinery, but some distance away. Demsing set off and said, "I don't know exactly where this Tudomany stays, but we're far enough down that we should pick up some trace of her."

"You're going to just step up to some innocent bystander and *ask* where she is?"

"Sure. We want to get there, and we want them to know we're going. Sure, we're bait, then, but it's the only way to find out. And besides, I have heard tales of this Tudomany ... it may well be worth the trip. I should warn you that if I have misjudged this, they may try to take you as a hostage to hold over me."

Chalmour started to speak as they walked toward the muttering sounds, the hum and buzz, but Demsing placed two fingers over her mouth. "No, no heroics! Absolutely none! Here, if you have been slack all your life, you must do exactly as I say, on faith. On this world, hostages are indeed kept, but they are almost never harmed, because dead or maimed, they have no value except revenge, and very few people want that turned loose."

Chalmour displayed an understanding of what Demsing was implying. "I see. All motives have natural limits, but revenge has none."

"And it ignites more in turn. So the possibility exists. A sharp operation could do it. I, like everyone else, have limits, and if they were willing to pay the price, they could do it. If that happens, behave yourself and wait patiently, I will not, no matter what, abandon you."

"Yes, I see that." She grasped Demsing's arm and pulled herself close to him. "But then you would compromise yourself, for me, and you must not do that. They want you, for whatever reasons. I have no value save as a coin to buy you."

"I have the distinct feeling that they don't want

that ... but there are always people of bad judgment everywhere who coast up to higher levels than they deserve, and you have to estimate for them. They make it hard for the rest of us."

Chalmour added, with a knife-edged cynicism that marked her for a true child of Teragon, "Right, just like all these *mouthy* people who talk honor, honor, more honor, and it turns out *they* have none themselves, and steer others by their calls to it."

Demsing nodded. "That's one of those catchwords that lead you to reach for your gun. There are a lot of them. I am glad you have learned that; some never do."

The corridor continued on, making several shallow turns, and finally opened up into a much larger space, almost a hall, which had echoes and an enormous high ceiling lost somewhere up in the shadows. Apparently at one time it had housed some sort of machinery, for marks were still on the *kamen* floor of metal foundations and the sheared-off bolts were still in the floor as well. At odd intervals, there were windows up in the walls, some frosted and translucent, others clear, some lighted, some not. Now it was used for a marketplace, everything from food and obviously new finished objects to the worst leavings of the thieves' markets. There seemed to be no order, no arrangement, just wherever the vendors could find space. Some had a lot, some had hardly any, and there was still a lot of space left, and the market was nowhere near working at capacity. There were few customers.

Demsing approached the first vendor they would

pass, an old man displaying bolts of cloth. Demsing showed the man a coin, but the vendor shook his head. They moved on to the next one, where Demsing showed the same coin to a group of urchins of about the same size and age as Fintry, but a lot less well-kept. They took the coin and began arguing over whose it was. Demsing made a complicated gesture, flamboyant, with his hand and seemed to pluck several more of the same sort of coin out of the air, which he held up for inspection.

"Tudomany the fortune teller." He waved the coins suggestively.

Two of them turned away and pretended to be interested in a set of enormous rusty stains on the near wall. The rest stared at him blankly. One finally said, "Elemezve the courtesan. On the farside, there." He pointed. "Give me the coins; I will see to a just distribution."

"We don't need courtesans."

"Ah, now, and who knows what they need? But if they needs Tudomany the Witch, Our Lady of the Sewers, they gots to aks Elemezve, they do, 'cos Tudy don't tell just anyone where she lies. That's the way it runs downhill."

Demsing handed over the coins, which immediately started an argument, all unintelligible, then, with Chalmour, set off across the hall in the direction the urchin had indicated.

Chalmour asked, "Is it all like this underground?"

Demsing glanced upwards, and said, "It gets worse. And, of course, there are a lot of empty areas, and other spaces where organized activity is carried out. There's plenty of room, but the view's not all that great."

Where the urchin had indicated, there was a large packing case laid on its side, and beyond it, another corridor, which was very dimly lit. They looked into the corridor, seeing nothing and suspecting that they had been swindled, but at that moment the end of the packing case creaked open, and a face peered out of it. A woman's face. Demsing thought that some faces showed evil, some showed goodness, some showed anger or lust. But this face showed none of these, only fatigue, endless years of it. It made him tired to look at her.

The face was followed by a heavyset body wreathed in swirling gauze veils whose color had faded. It announced, "I am Elemezve. What are your needs? Aha, a pair of them! They need novelty, education, instruction, entertainment! I can provide them all! All positions, all permutations, including those known only to trained religious atheletes." She pushed the crate-end open all the way, to reveal a blowsy den full of antique lamps, print curtains, and astrological mandalas juxtaposed with sexual instructional diagrams, illustrated by photographs of somber models engaged in the utmost degree of seriousness. A sign on the wall proclaimed, with true sporting intent, "I no come forth, you must pay; I come forth, you no pay; I come forth twice, I pay you."

Demsing smiled, "You are a true gambler! I salute you!"

Elemezve observed where his attention was and agreed, expansively, "It is the motto of my business! One may not live by avarice alone: it stifles the loins and clabbers the bowels. In addition to the usual performances, I also offer The Wall Job, The Knot Job, the Pearl Trick, The Birdcage. . . ."

Chalmour interrupted, "I beg your pardon, but do you have a menu?"

Elemezve pulled her head back in astonishment. "Oh, now! If you could have heard just what I've seen."

Demsing glanced back over his shoulder, where the urchins had vanished, and others were starting to pick through their flea-market offerings, and then back to Elemezve. "I am a student of the Holy Tantra and will pass on further instruction for the moment; however I do need to find a lady called Tudomany, or Tudy."

The aged courtesan smiled knowingly. "I see, I know. But it is unfair to use magic on a girl who has aleady surrendered without it."

Chalmour's face darkened visibly, even in the uncertain and indirect light of the hall. Demsing continued, "The boys over there suggested you might exchange some directions."

Elemezve seemed to reflect for a time, as if pondering the theory of Quantum Gravitation, but this also had the air of a worn-out stage gesture. Finally she said, as if into the air, "Tudomany is retired and does not, to my knowledge, take on new accounts."

He said quietly, "I have heard much the same tale topside; but I also bring the news that Tudomany may be able to resolve peculiar questions which no one up there is interested in."

Elemczve performed an odd little dance-in-place. "Just so! Just So! None of them is interested in the least in the vital issues of life, where one's very foundations lie! They sail along and thrust the unfortunate below, but what they need, they come along. Tudomany could very well be dead. Long ago! Then what should they do for the so-called irrationals they don't wish to bother with, I ask you!"

Demsing said, "The problem is mine, and there is no one up there I trust to answer it."

"I quite understand. I am Tudomany. Come in." And instantly, as if she had been making her evaluation, a mask fell away and a persona rather different from the blown rose of the old courtesan appeared. She added, "Those boys do not know."

Demsing said back, "They will soon enough. We don't have much time."

The old woman responded, "I know that, too, as I saw what was between you two. Come. Sit. Speak of these things. Tell me your tale."

7

In the parlance of the Intelligence Community, a city is a place where Lines of Communication intersect in a manner that enables quanta from one line to shift to another, or others. A Line of Communication can be anything along which something flows: electronic impulses, ideas, bulk substances, finished goods, money, food. The City is an artifact of these processes, not the creator of them, and derives its reason for existence from this meaningful interaction. We have worked with diligence to reach this point, but it is a beginning, not a summation, and a tool, not a result.

H. C., The Illusions of Form

The place was one of the infrequent dance halls where people could find some transitory release from the unending and unrelenting pressure of Teragon. Not that the pressure was intense, by any absolute measurement—it wasn't in actual fact. In truth, at its upper measure, the density of pressure on Teragon was about a third of what it could be on certain planets and certain societies. The problem on Teragon was that the maximum and the minimum were the same. There was no variation, no release, no letup and, in essence, no slack.

The basic beat of the dance was provided by a Drum Machine and a Bass Tone Sequencer pumping out a very basic progression in 5/4 time, to which live musicians provided words, basic chants, squeals, grunts, and short but poignant solo runs and breaks, and the dancers provided the motions, more grunts, and considerable sweat, even in the decidedly cool air of Teragon. To the untrained ear it sounded very mechanical at first, but after a time one could begin to perceive the subtle *ritards* and anticipations, the syncopation behind the beat, and the excursions into backbeat and prebeat provided by a live Bass player, who played circles around the Sequencer with contemptuous ease. In addition, the basic rhythm would shift from 5/4 to a combination of 4/4 mixed with 6/4, which produced an odd pattern of cadences and kept the dancers alert.

It was also a place where the ancient codes of body language flowed and rippled over the dancers, the musicians, and idlers who stopped by to watch, with an unending panorama of sexual messages whose content ranged from the near side of innocent exaltations of healthy young bodies all the way to unspeakable, incomprehensible corruptions. It was also the most perfectly camouflaged location on Teragon for the open transmission of information by subtle modifications of body motion.

Thelledy viewed her own life as one of monastic discipline and the intense exertion of will to the limits of human ability. Whatever the appearance was to the outside world, within the discipline of the Wa'an School life was a hard and grim reality without much release. The Dance halls provided what release there was, and an excellent opportunity for communication between field operatives and key decision-makers within the Wa'an structure, and that was exactly what she was doing now. In the actual flow of information, the effect was that of a high-speed conversation among several participants, some of whom were not even on the floor. It was, for Thelledy, both the most demanding activity she could imagine, and an incredible release at the same time.

Her major partner was a wiry young man she knew as Ilyen, who moved like a serpent, but there were others in the net: a nearby couple known to her as Cellila and Meldogast—both stocky and powerful in their movements—and a watcher off the dance floor, a woman of mature appearance called Telny.

Their motions, rhythms, and convolutions made up, a form of communication which flowed like speech among them, and provided an information environment considerably quieter and more noise-free than the normal range of human speech. The motions of the others, dancing their hearts out, created, within this system, random noise of low volume which was reduced by the discipline to a distant dull muttering, like a light surf on a beach.

THELLEDY: As I outlined in my request for this meeting, the subject Demsing continues to follow what is for him an irrational course.

MELDOGAST: Current location?

THELLEDY: He and the girl have made contact with Tudomany.

CELLILA: They made no concealment?

TELNY: Demsing has never performed a direct action since we have had him under observation.

MELDOGAST: This action then is concealment for something else.

ILYEN: Or is irrational, or else may be a direct action for other undetermined purposes.

THELLEDY: No evasive action. They went directly there.

MELDOGAST: The girl Chalmour is also uncharacteristic.

THELLEDY: That was the reason for my initial alert.

TELNY: Galitzyn is aware of these events?

ILYEN: Affirmative. He has been kept informed.

TELNY: His reactions?

THELLEDY: Fear.

TELNY: Demsing is aware of his surveillance, and of our contact with Galitzyn. This has been demonstrated.

CELLILA: In that light, then, this action is an open provocation.

THELLEDY: Exactly. But to what end?

TELNY: Obvious. He wants to see someone make a more obvious move.

MELDOGAST: Then we should not respond.

TELNY: That does not necessarily follow. The evaluation by the Advisory Board is that if no one makes a move, he will take the girl and vanish.

THELLEDY: Galitzyn also has fear of that. He and his people have made repeated references to 'untimely activation.'

CELLILA: We have seen several references to that. Activate what?

THELLEDY: Demsing has something he himself is currently unaware of. We have not been able to recover the nature of this possession.

TELNY: It is not a physical object of macroscopic dimension. Therefore it is abstract: knowledge or an ability.

MELDOGAST: He has put us all in a nice quandary.

TELNY: He has very neatly taken the initiative.

CELLILA: This contingency was considered as a possible outcome of the Asztali operation.

TELNY: The Board assigned a lower probability to that. The conclusion must be that Demsing is potentially more dangerous than our estimates, though for everyone else our predictions appear to remain accurate.

ILYEN: We must not be used in this manner.

TELNY: We have lost many choices we might have preferred.

THELLEDY: Is Demsing a potential threat to us?

TELNY: He has the potential. To date, he has not revealed any such intent.

CELLILA: This unknown possession of his remains an unevaluated threat.

MELDOGAST: The fears of others are often instructive.

THELLEDY: Galitzyn is a poor operative, despite what he thinks he knows.

CELLILA: The fears of a wimp lead to no answers.

MELDOGAST: Can we derive information from this Galitzyn?

THELLEDY: He has the signs of Deathreflex protection.

MELDOGAST: What, then, of Chalmour?

TELNY: Chalmour is a complication.

ILYEN: We have no charter nor reason to press Demsing.

MELDOGAST: He killed Asztali.

CELLILA: Demsing terminated a mistake we all share in.

TELNY: Demsing released Asztali from her obligations in an honorable manner.

MELDOGAST: I understand well enough that if we do nothing, Demsing will vanish and attempt to recover this possession on his own.

CELLILA: Assuming he suspects.

THELLEDY: He suspects. He has left an obvious trail.

MELDOGAST: What about Faren Kiricky?

ILYEN: Protected by arrangement with the Water Cabal.

MELDOGAST: But she knows.

TELNY: She knows. But she has spent her life concealing it from Demsing.

THELLEDY: What she knows is less than Galitzyn. We know that.

CELLILA: Does she fear Demsing?

ILYEN: No. She fears for him.

MELDOGAST: That is extremely interesting.

THELLEDY: He is trailing Chalmour plainly as a target.

ILYEN: That is why we must not reach for her. We can expect a trap.

TELNY: Chalmour is our only key. His actions state that clearly. Direct your operatives to pick her up before we completely lose control of this.

THELLEDY: Galitzyn will not like this.

CELLILA: The tasking says we are not to. . . .

TELNY: Galitzyn is relatively unimportant now.

THELLEDY: That may be difficult.

TELNY: Pick up the girl unharmed. Absolutely. No experiments. And no interrogation. She is to be our envoy. And see that he sees that.

THELLEDY: He already knows that. This will cost a lot of people.

TELNY: Then use expendables.

THELLEDY: What about Tudomany?

TELNY: Taken alive. Interrogated.

ILYEN: What about her role underground?

TELNY: Cellila will replace her as wisewoman. Use workname Jollensie.

CELLILA: I hear.

ILYEN: Why are we taking this action?

TELNY: Demsing is generating too many unknowns. We have to know, so we may deal with this in an appropriate manner.

THELLEDY: What about Galitzyn?

TELNY: You know nothing. Demsing has ordinary enemies.

THELLEDY: I hear.

TELNY: Central is in contact with me. The order is do it now.

MELDOGAST: Demsing must be kept from Galit-zyn at all cost.

TELNY: I concur.

Suddenly Telny dropped out of the net, and in response, the entire net fell silent. They all remained, though, waiting. Thelledy hesitated a fraction of a second, considering possibilities, and not finding much comfort in them, but she did as she had been instructed, nevertheless, and dropping out of the net, she made a series of gestures to a relay-man off on another part of the floor who was blind to the net motional language they had used, but highly tuned to her specific operations. The message was simple and direct, and took less than thirty standard seconds to transmit. It took another sixty to retransmit those instructions to another relay-man, who picked up a telephone, waited for the other end to pick up, and spoke one word into the mouthpiece.

It was at that point that the series of events assumed a momentum of its own.

What Demsing told Tudomany was a strange tale of a lifetime of inexplicable hallucinations which felt like memories but logically could not be. He also told of learning how to perform certain actions much easier than he thought he could, and learning to conceal this at an early age. And more, of a growing ability to perceive the true structure of events around him on what he himself considered to be too few clues.

Tudomany settled back in a pile of ornamental

cushions and asked, "Why would you question such a gift?"

"Because I don't know its source, and what else of it there might be. But I would not have questioned it, if it had not come to my attention that I was being followed by the Wa'an School, in conjunction with a planted offworlder posing as an Archivist. Until then, I had just accepted it and used as much of it as I could. But after that, I wondered. . . . I mean, until then, I could explain it away as any number of things, but the conclusion is unavoidable that there is something there, and others know about it, and seem to be trying to reach something."

"You don't see purpose behind this?"

"Not yet."

"Wa'an School . . . Those are not so good to have as shadows. What do you think they know?"

"Their actions suggest a pattern within which they are working under a very tight contract, going on very little factual information. I have not tested this theory, but it rings true."

Tudomany looked off, and then at one of the illustrated positions tacked on the faded walls. She said, musing into space, "Other than what you call operational necessity, you have not tried to explore this thing in yourself?"

"No. In a sense, I have not believed in it. I have been living under the arbitrary assumption . . ."

"So do we all."

". . . that this was not real, and an attempt to explore it would endanger me needlessly."

"I can understand that. Well . . . you can do

several things. You could always arrange to confront your suspect Archivist with a simple direct question—'who am I and why do you want me, and what will you pay for it?' Something like that."

"They don't want negotiation, and they don't want to buy it: they want a certain level of control."

Chalmour, who had been quiet, now hissed, "They want to give orders and have the flunkies jump, but they don't want to be responsible for what happens!"

Demsing agreed, "Yes, that, too. I think that they fear whatever it is and want to have some control over how it emerges."

Tudomany snorted, "That's nothing new! The bastards fear everything they don't understand, even simple things ordinary people learn to do. Well, I suggest that, but I don't think you'll get very far. So the alternative is to go within and go exploring until you find the key, and then unlock it. If you dare."

"Oh, if I have it, I'll use it. It's looking for it that's the daring part."

Chalmour said, guardedly, "Is that. . . . ?"

Demsing said, "No. It was not calculated. It was only after I learned how much we trusted each other that it became possible to consider it." Here he stopped. "But . . . I don't know what I'll be, and there are things I don't want changed, now."

Chalmour looked at him long and hard, and said, "Do it. I will take my chances, after hearing that. You'll remember. You have to believe in something, and you have to test that faith."

Tudomany said, "There you have it. What more could you ask?"

"Nothing."

"But not here. No, not here, not now. Get somewhere where you can take the time to do it right, and where you can be helped if you fail. In fact, you are in danger here, I . . ."

Demsing stopped her as well as Chalmour with a raised finger, and then indicated they were to be silent.

Tudomany asked, softly, "What?"

Demsing said, even more softly, "There was a constant noise out in the hall as we came to it, and when we came here. It stopped just a moment ago."

Chalmour sat up suddenly. "It's now!"

He asked, "How do we get out of this box?"

Tudomany smiled at this and struggled to her feet, reaching for a large picture-book. She did something to the title, touching the ornamental letters in a certain sequence, and then laid the book down. Then she scuffed a rug aside and pointed to a trapdoor. Demsing lifted it and saw a square access plate, which he lifted also.

Tudomany whispered, "Quick, now!"

Demsing motioned Chalmour into the black hole below, a shaft leading somewhere unknown. After a moment, she stepped onto the rungs and began climbing down with surprising agility. Demsing followed her, and after him, with unexpected agility, came the bulk of Tudomany, who arranged the hatches.

In the total darkness, she hissed down the shaft,

"That won't hold them up long—they'll see the hatch. But I left them a surprise."

"The Book?"

"Exactly." She stopped, hearing a grating noise from above, and a sudden commotion, as of many persons suddenly rushing into the box. There was silence while the intruders obviously looked about the empty packing-case with consternation, and then another hubbub as someone noticed the trap-door. Tudomany called down to them, "Fast, now! They found it!"

There came another sliding noise, and a metallic sound, and at the top of the shaft, a bright square light, yellowish like Tudomany's lamps, illuminated the shaft, and then there was a sharp, stabbing blue flash, and the metal panel slammed shut with a painful ringing clang, which was completely covered over even as it rang in their ears by the unmistakable roar of a demolition grenade. Flakes and particles rained down on them in the shaft.

Tudomany called down, "That will give us a little time, now, so downwards, my children, waste no time. This goes a long way down and there aren't many exits, and we won't use them. All the way to the bottom, and keep it quiet."

The climb down the shaft was in darkness and silence; padding on the rungs reduced any sound they might have made. In addition, the unusual position of the descent, and the use of muscle groups not normally used, made the extended downward climb tiring and demanding; there was no conversation, not even about which way to go, since

Tudomany had plainly said "All the way to the bottom," and that was that.

There were some unidentifiable noises, mostly faint and far away, sometimes emanating from side-tubes which they passed occasionally, or from deeper down. The message of the noises was clear to Demsing; that however deep they were, there was more farther down.

As they descended, Chalmour's supple, agile body suffered least from the strain of the climb and she lengthened her lead on Demsing, while Tudomany, not at all suited to this kind of exercise, quickly fell behind, with the result that Demsing found himself mostly alone, with only an occasional scrape or rattle identifying the girl below him or the woman above. Soon, the motions of climbing became almost automatic, and he had time to think about where he was and what they were doing.

They had certainly taken the bait. The response had been faster than he had expected, and considerably stronger. That was powerful information, because it told him definitely that whatever it was he concealed, they didn't want him finding it on his own. Demsing chuckled silently to himself on that one: that was nothing new, just a slightly more powerful version of a much older idea. People who surrendered to organizations tended to suppress self-discovery of any kind, even trivial manifestations of it.

Demsing had some question as to who it might have been, but he felt fairly certain that the attack had come from Thelledy's group. How much they were acting on behalf of their client, Galitzyn and whomever he represented, remained questionable. Indeed, as he thought about it, it seemed less Galitzyn and more Thelledy. That was not a considered estimate, or even what he would have called a perception, but a characteristic feel of the way it had gone. He made a mental note to explore that in detail, later, when they had reached wherever Tudomany was leading them.

And where would that be? Below a certain level, Demsing's knowledge of the underworld of Teragon fell off rapidly. For the most part, the inhabitants of Teragon favored the surface, accepting its dim daylight and impossible local time as minor inconveniences, as opposed to delving deeply into the lower regions. No one Demsing knew had systematically explored the underside. Certain parts of it were known, and used, more or less regularly; many of the industrial processes were underground, and all of the necessary functional industries, such as the food production plants, fermenteries, and hydroponic tanks, where the atmosphere of Teragon was presumably recycled, and the water extracted.

Those things were known, more or less, according to who used such information. But no one knew the full extent of the underworld. In general, the deeper one went, the more localized became the transportation systems, so people who went under for their own reasons were far more local in their movements than the surface-dwellers.

One thing was known about it, which seemed to be true all over the planet. The oxygen content of the atmosphere decreased slightly as one went down, and the Carbon Dioxide content went up.

And since the main component of the atmosphere was known to be Argon* in the deeper levels the pressure increased and the temperature did also.

These were generalities, which were useless in specific situations. All he knew was that they were going down an unspecified distance, where, presumably they would be free of pursuit, and able to gain some time.

At rare intervals, he would come to a small landing, which seemed to be nothing more than a shelf and a junction with other shafts, some of which were larger, some smaller. Down, she had said, and so he continued, reassured by occasional calls from above and below, as Chalmour, ahead, and Tudomany, behind, passed through the same points. Demsing continued down.

At last, after what had seemed like an eternity of climbing, his arms and the backs of his thighs starting to burn and sting, he stepped down for a rung and felt solid *kamen* underfoot.

Wherever he was, there had been no sense of transition from the shaft to the space. He had been climbing down, and then the shaft ended. The air was, to his senses, dense and still, but not dead

---

*The atmosphere of Teragon at the surface displayed the following constituent percentages: 51% Argon, 25% Oxygen (in the form O_2. A shallow layer above the surface of O_3, Ozone, accounted for another 1% of total Oxygen volume), 1% Ozone, Nitrogen 12%, 3% Carbon Dioxide, 7% Neon, 1% Water Vapor and other trace elements and compounds. The nominal standard pressure at the surface is 610 Millibars, which is equivalent to Earth-standard altitudes of approximately 11,000 to 12,000 feet.

air. This chamber opened onto other areas. And, though he did not notice it immediately, he could tell there was no one in it except him. Furthermore, there was obviously no one in the shaft above him. Somewhere in the shaft, both Tudomany and Chalmour had been taken without a sound.

8

In the seventies, a famous experiment was conducted in which researchers, disguised as psychopaths who had been committed to that institution, penetrated a certain psychiatric institution. These sane people were never discovered by the staff, even when they acted normally. (One of the favorite diagnoses was "Flight into Normality.") And of course that was the whole purpose of the experiment. What was totally unexpected was the serendipitous discovery that the inmates, the real psychopaths, knew the difference immediately without aids or clues, and identified the false psychopaths without visible logical deductive processes.

There are available a large number of conclusions which one might draw from this, or jump to as the case might be; but being suspicious and cynical of expressed motivations as I am, I cannot avoid concluding that the victims always perceive that they are being jerked around by callous manipulators, and that even psychopaths can see through a line of buzzword shuck and jive. Perhaps we might even suspect that is why they are as they are. And if we suspect that sanity is the perception, comprehension, and

functional integration of reality, then we may
ask, indeed, who are the sane, and who are the
basket cases?

—H. C. Attitude Papers

Chalmour plainly did not know where she was,
and hadn't since she had been taken in the shaft.
There had been no time to call out: at a cross-shaft
junction, she had been snatched to one side as
another had soundlessly slipped into her place.
She had been held in an odd hold, with pressure
applied at certain points, which had made it impossible to speak. She had tried. Nothing worked.

They had let Demsing pass before they moved
on, somewhere unknown, reached through a maze
of tunnels and shafts they had traversed in silence
and almost total darkness, with a lot of turns and
climbs seemingly thrown in for added confusion.
She had understood then that it was useless to try
to navigate in her head, and had concentrated on
keeping her mind carefully blank and receptive,
ready to untangle what would finally be presented
to it.

It was pleasing to her to see Demsing's predic-
tion come true with such ease: They neither harmed
her nor molested her during the long journey, and
when they reached wherever they were, they had
shut her up in—not a cell—but a decent room with
facilities. The facilities—running water and a
toilet—were decoration. The room was impregna-
ble, as best as she could determine.

Initially, they shut her in and left her alone, all

in total silence, and in darkness as well. She thought she had heard a faint, dry, sliding sound, like short sequences of raspy chattering nearby, and supposed that they communicated with each other by means of a touch-code: fingers met in a pattern of pressures, taps, and slides. But although she knew such things existed, she didn't know any herself, and couldn't read *theirs*.

For a while, they left her in the dark. Chalmour explored the room with her fingers and soon had an accurate representation of it in her mind. It was small and plain and there were no traps or movable walls. It was just a room with a door which locked from the outside. The ceiling was out of reach for her, standing, but she could jump and touch it, and it was as solid as the rest. That kept her busy for a long time, because she was not adept, but they appeared to give her plenty of time, and she used it as best she could.

Also, she listened, and felt for vibrations in the walls and floor. At first she felt and heard nothing, but she expected that. As the time wore on, her senses became more sensitive, and she began to pick up faint sounds and weak vibrations. Demsing had talked to her about this, but had only shown her certain basic exercises. Now she learned as she went, and learned to perceive through the noise her own body made, creaks and snaps of joints, low rumbles of muscles, her heartbeat and breathing, swallowing, and the rumbles of her digestive tract. It was that quiet. But she waited, and presently some things began to appear. Not so near, she heard a soft, thudding vibration, fairly frequent, but at odd intervals in a rhythm and pattern she could not quite identify. As her senses sharpened, she detected a suggestion of movement to this vibration, and tentatively identified it as of the Linduc line. They had not crossed it on the surface, and it seemed off to the side, very slightly higher than the horizontal.

She learned to feel people walking. That one was very dull and blurred-out and impossible to follow, but she could tell there were several by the way they overlapped. And there were faint sounds, too: conversations too weak and far-off to resolve, but perceptible enough for her to guess at how many there were, and where. The footfalls were connected with her, and so was one set of the muttering conversations. Another set, somewhat fainter, seemed to have no relation to her, nor did any other noises. That one, she adjudged to be a living area or work area a little farther off. She was near the surface, and gravity told her which way was up.

Demsing had told her: *Use the time! Never sit idle. Listen, feel, walk around. Work on making a picture. And don't worry or anticipate. They want you bored and sensory-deprived. Keep busy! Make up an imaginary language and conjugate verbs in it! Invent a non-decimal number system and hunt for Prime Numbers. Memorize the results. And pace yourself. Sleep if you feel like it, and know the difference between sleep and waking. Stimulate yourself sexually—it's fun and it breaks a tension they damn sure want you to have. Explore chord progressions in music. And learn the basic routine pattern of where you are and who is there. And then watch for the breaks in the flow. Learn to use that and it will tell you a lot more than they want you to know. If you see a break, go for it. Nine times out of ten it's a real opportunity. The odds actually favor you. Prisoners are their own best guards, repeating to themselves, 'I can't.'*

Chalmour also knew about the old trick of wetting your hands, cooling them by blowing on them, and feeling about for Infra-red emitters. As far as she could tell, there were none, although the room was warmer than the usual Teragon chill, but the warmth seemed to come solely from a hot water pipe to the washbasin.

And he had said, And if they ask about me, tell them whatever you know. Because you don't know what they want to know; I don't know it, either, so you couldn't know it.

She smirked to herself in the dark. *This could wind up being less of a bother than a trip to the dentist.* There was, of course, another way it could go, equally probable, but that she only considered long enough to make herself know that it existed. That was sufficient.

She knew that her perception of Time would be distorted and magnified, so for a long stretch she ignored the seemingly endless passage of hours. Eventually, however, she felt hunger pangs, which she put off by drinking water, which she smelled carefully before drinking it. As far as she could tell, it was just plain tap water, put there to drink. The toilet worked, flushing with a deafening industrial-strength roar which she found extremely funny. She even thought of telling them, when they eventually arrived, that they should be careful what they put in it: it charged when wounded. But she later decided not to, because that remark would reveal the nature of her defenses—and that Thelledy thought that she had been clumsy. She'd show her, and in such a way that Thelledy would know it only after she had gone.

And so Thelledy: Chalmour never questioned who was behind this, and expected to confront Thelledy herself whenever her captors appeared. Therefore she was a little disappointed when footfalls outside stopped at her door. A small lamp lit in a wall alcove, and a panel slid open, revealing dim light outside. A man, rather young by the sound of his voice, said, "Dinnertime," and slid a tray in with hot food. She mumbled a muffled gratitude, surprised at her creaky voice, and the unseen young man slid in a package through the opening. "Here's some fresh clothes, too. It may be a little warm in there for what you have." He sounded pleasant enough, and seemed to be going to some trouble to avoid a threatening appearance. But she only thanked him and said nothing else, though her mind was boiling with questions. She thought it an extraordinary piece of self-discipline: Demsing had told her: *Never, never ask anything! Questions reveal more than answers!*

The food was better than average, and tasted good. She had no ill effects from it. After she ate, she washed the tray and the spoon they had provided, and then looked at the clothing. The light remained on; although rather dim, it was a vast improvement over total darkness. In the light, the clothing appeared to be a loose caftan made of soft cloth. It was a dull neutral brown in color, and was of no specific size, although she could wear it without doing too much to it. Without hesitating, she stripped, put it on, washed her old clothing out, and draped it over the end of the bunk to dry. Then, pleased with herself, she lay down on the bunk to relax, and took a nap with her arms propped behind her head.

"Psht! But you're a cool one!"

It woke Chalmour up, and her head cleared instantly. She had been asleep, but not very deep, not dreaming; now someone was in the room with her, and the time had come.

She opened her eyes, but made no move. The voice was familiar, the same one who had brought the tray earlier. This resolved into a slender young man slightly taller than herself, so she estimated, wearing a loose caftan similar to the one she had on, the one they had given her. His was a very dark blue, almost black. *What does that tell you? That wherever you are, there's a distinctive dress worn internally, that they can spot you instantly, and that if you escape, they can pick you out of a crowd. Thank you, Demsing.* Chalmour risked a quick glance around the room, at nothing in particular, but including the foot of the bunk in its sweep: her clothes were gone, sure enough.

She sat up, rubbing her eyes, and swung her feet over the side. "Would you run that by me again?"

"I said, you were cool and collected for one who

was just pulled out of an air shaft on her way somewhere."

She shrugged. "I was tired; I took a nap."

It seemed to put him off, as if he had been prepared for another response. He waited a moment, and then said, "I am Ilyen. Mainly why I am here is to reassure you that you are not in any danger. You might consider this protective custody, temporary in nature."

"I see."

"Is there anything I can get you? Books, handicrafts?"

"Out."

For a moment, he stepped back, as if her ambiguous reply had confused him. "What do you want?"

"I want out, in the simplest possible way of saying it. If you can't do that, then get out."

For a fraction of a second, something utterly dark and maleficent flickered across his face, a narrowing of the eyes, a tightening of the mouth, but it was gone almost before she could see it, and the bland expression returned. He said, quite evenly, and Chalmour admired his control, "Well, actually, I'm as much compelled by circumstance as you find yourself, so that is quite beyond me at the moment. But I will bring you such items as you would like to have. Also I will take the tray back. And later, when I bring the things you want back, we might converse for a little."

Chalmour stared fixedly at the toilet, and said, in a monotone, "You have the key; come and go as you will. If you insist on bringing something, then bring a folio copy of *Malinoski's Contrapunctus Semidecimus*; I should like to review my exercises."

He picked up the tray and gave a slight, stiff bow. "I am not familiar with the work you mention, but I will see if I can obtain a copy; we have an excellent library." For a moment, he stopped, uncertainly. Then he asked, sheepishly, "To what does this volume refer?"

"Musical theory and chord progression." And as Ilyen reached for the door to leave, she added, "And when you come back, knock first, will you?"

The door closed behind him and locked automatically, a fact Chalmour did not miss; she smirked, suppressing a giggle. She had improvised on one of Demsing's principles: the work she had asked for was imaginary, and she thought that it might give them some difficulty. She had no idea how much difficulty this actually did cause.

As she measured time, it wasn't very long until Ilyen returned, and to her surprise, he did knock before he unlocked the door. Needless to say, he had no book with him. He was dressed as before, and carried about him an air composed of subtle wariness, which had not been there before, and a curious shy wistfulness which made him rather more attractive.

He opened the conversation, apologetically, "I was unable to obtain it. Are you certain such a volume exists?"

"Oh, it exists, all right. It is as real as your reasons for holding me."

"It must be uncommon. We could find no reference to it."

"I worked with a private copy. It is a very old work. Possibly your index is incomplete."

Ilyen nodded, agreeably, "It is certainly possible. Never fear! We are unrelenting and will get to the bottom of it, eventually."

Chalmour understood the remark perfectly, and the threat it represented. She decided it was time to be more bland with them. "What would you like to discuss? Here, sit on the edge of the bed; if you have to be here, you might as well be comfortable."

"Some of us have expressed a certain curiosity about a person called Demsing, who sometimes uses the surname Ngellathy; we have a certain interest in your relationship with him, and some general things you might know about him."

"That seems a large list."

Ilyen sat on the end of the bed. "You do have a certain association with him?"

Chalmour was quite impatient with this pussy-footing, but she answered, "I could hardly avoid such association. He was given duty as chief of apprentices over the group of apprentices to which I belong."

"Who made the assignment?"

"Klippisch assigned Demsing to that duty; Thelledy volunteered myself out of her group. Myself, and Fintry, that is."

Ilyen stretched; she caught the nagged motion out of the corner of her eye. He seemed to relax a little more, and asked, "But there is more to it than that."

Chalmour wondered about this line of questioning; surely they already knew this. Or perhaps it was more an exercise to allow her to babble on. It didn't matter, because she didn't, she thought, know anything, and perhaps by talking she could occupy their attention. And waste their time. She said, pensively, "Yes, there was more."

"What?" *Was this idiot a total cretin?*

"I found him attractive and went to bed with him. He made no resistance and seemed to enjoy himself. We continued the relationship because it became pleasant. It's really simple."

"I understand that simplicity." Ilyen leaned back so that he displayed his slender grace to advantage. It caught her attention, however much she disliked the situation she was in, which he represented. It was as if she had two minds. He added, "Did this cause any problem in the job to which Demsing was assigned?"

"No. He seemed to evaluate each of us according to what he thought we could do, and then suited the exercises he gave us to that. He was all work, and that's the way it was; I understood that and practiced no public displays. What we did, he and I, we did in free time." She felt oddly relieved as she said this.

"Would you continue this, if free to do so?"

"We have made arrangements to make it permanent."

"Yes, of course." He stretched again, a subtle and slight motion, and looked at her intently. She saw that the questions didn't really matter. They already knew all this.

Ilyen turned on his side, facing her, and said, "You have had other lovers?"

Oddly, she didn't find this offensive. "Yes."

"How were they?"

"Some were good, some not so good, some very good. None were bad." She felt lazy, relaxed, and sensual. A lassitude was creeping into her limbs. She saw it happening, as if from outside. She thought, *I don't want to do this, but I don't seem to be able to stop it. What the hell is he doing to me and how is he doing it?* Ilyen had only a small distance to reach across to touch her knee, did so, casually, and she did not move her leg. Perhaps she could have; she didn't know. She didn't try. Nor did she raise any objection to what followed, seemingly naturally and easily enough, and very slowly, too. She remembered that. And the part of her that didn't object enjoyed it very much. It lasted a long time, that wiry, agile body joined to hers, and, to the part of her that did object, incredibly, she asked him to stay. He reassured her he would return often.

After he left, she allowed herself to become very angry. But even that took a long time. And with the anger came fear, too. *If he can do that to me so easily, and he does come back, how long can I hold up against that.* And she added, *Those bastards know I don't know anything, so what Ilyen's doing is just playing with me. I'm nothing to them but bait: they'll keep me alive, fed, and well-laid, and it's some trick he's learned how to do, like Thelledy. And if I throw him out, they'll send one even better, or worse, depending on how you look at it.* Now she understood Demsing's lessons, some of which she had taken rather lightly. *The real enemy was the despair you felt yourself when you realized how much power those people had. What did he have to resist them?*

Ilyen opened the door to a small room similar to the one he had just left, but this one held no toilet, there was no lock on the door, and there were two people inside waiting for his analysis: Thelledy and Telny.

Thelledy said, "You took long enough."

Telny glanced at the younger woman, but said nothing.

Ilyen answered, carefully, "Chalmour has no defenses whatsoever against skills we take for granted." He shook his head. "She rather enjoyed herself, and wanted more."

Telny observed, "That's very interesting. You mean Demsing has taught her nothing about projection and control?"

"Apparently not. She seems to have no defenses. Additionally, she knows little or nothing. He seems to have revealed nothing to her that we don't already know; that he's extraordinarily adept and perceptive. We are not going to get an answer from her as to why they want him."

Telny said, "Nor out of that Tudomany, either. She didn't know Demsing from *reclama**. Told him

---

*Reclama is the combined slurry which is recycled and fractionated into basic chemical components. In effect, sewage, although reclama is considerably more complicated than that.

to seek answers inside himself, that's what she did. We tried to dig deeper, but she was obviously working for somebody, because she activated a very crude deathlock which beat us very neatly. Dead end there, and no pun. Lost her."

Ilyen breathed deeply, and said, "It occurs to me that we could wind up with a problem, holding Chalmour."

Telny questioned this. "How so?"

"Demsing is considered a formidable individual with informal skills which approach the levels of the best of formal systems, and, from our file material on him, he has a wider range than do members of formalistic disciplines. He can be a dangerous and destructive adversary, as he stands. Now, from other sources, we come to understand that there may be some unknown quantity related to him, which has unknown consequences. And we elect to challenge him directly ... and hold a girl as a hostage, so to speak, whom he has selected. ..."

Thelledy interrupted, "Ilyen, I cannot find fault with your summary, except in this very soft area of Demsing and Chalmour. That is a soft area because we cannot comprehend the reasons behind it. That is what is disturbing, so we continue to search. Chalmour must be the leading edge of that probe."

Ilyen responded, with a faint aura of anger well-hidden, "That is what I am trying to tell you: we may be looking for something which may not exist. While we manufacture imaginary mythology, Demsing erects a system in reality which we don't anticipate because we can't imagine it. I have tested Chalmour and my evaluation is that there is nothing hidden in her. Nothing. I suspect very strongly that that is precisely the reason Demsing has responded to her, and. . . ."

Thelledy interrupted again, "If you open that door. . . ."

Telny made a slight hand motion which stopped Thelledy. She said, pointedly, to Ilyen, "Your line of thinking interests me."

Thelledy countered, "He is not being paid to think, but to act. All he does is serve as a challenge target* for field agents such as myself . . ."

Telny turned, slowly, until she was facing Thelledy directly, and paused for emphasis, allowing all of them to recognize the taut physique, the short, closely trimmed gray hair, and the controlled bearing that characterized Telny and her rank within the Wa'an School. She said nothing for a long time. Finally she said, slowly, "Good ideas are not intrinsically coupled to a given source. Intelligence and stupidity are equal in that: they may occur anywhere. Ilyen, continue your exposition."

"As I may have implied, Chalmour was easy because she has no defensive procedures to protect

---

*A challenge target was a person who served, by analogy, as a sort of sparring partner, by which an operative might practice skills, techniques, and routines. It was assumed that the target would be of high skill level, but of necessity slightly lower than the main operatives. In the context of the Wa'an School, such a person might be assigned to "service" as many as five to ten field agents such as Thelledy.

her against advanced psychosexual manipulations carried out by someone trained in their use, at whatever level. Very well. *Because* of this, there is a very great danger that continued application of the techniques can and probably will cause psychological damage to her which may not be treatable in the context of Teragon. Yes, it was easy. But only because during such manipulation, her mind divides into two parts and she fights herself without knowing what the true source of the conflict is. Under the manipulation, she is deeply oriented toward Demsing and from what I could detect of the far side of *that*, he appears to be oriented toward her in similar fashion."

Telny looked up, into space, thoughtfully. "You can *feel* Demsing?"

"Yes. Weak, but definite. I used Alcinoë's Perceptor, in the third mode, and all confirmations fit the receptor sites."

Telny mused, "Then you understand the consequences of that? No? I shall explain: If she is that transparent to him, then he is also transparent to her. They have removed all defenses and blocks. This is significant and important, and we must follow it out. It is a rare condition."

Whatever train of thought Telny was following was interrupted by a soft knock at the door, followed by a messenger, a slight girl with close-cropped curly hair. The girl said, "I have information for Lodgemaster Telny."

"Speak."

"A followup search was conducted and the where-abouts of the subject, one each Demsing Ngellathy, are not known."

Telny responded instantly, "Instruct the field agents to increase their efforts. Have the agent in charge of operations to request negotiation with Demsing on contact. Send this message: 'Chalmour to be returned to you as soon as we know your location, no questions asked, request consultation. Urgent.' Repeat it back to me."

The girl did as instructed. Telny told her, "Go now."

The girl left, and Telny turned her attention again to Ilyen. "Who directed you to seduce Chalmour?"

Ilyen did not hesitate. "Thelledy."

Telny nodded. "Too late to undo that. See that it does not occur again, under my personal seal, no excuses, your sole responsibility direct to me. Understood?"

"Yes."

She turned to Thelledy. "You will make contact with Galitzyn and derive what we are looking for from him. Use standard contract Clause Five: Suspect danger, will void contract unless information is provided."

Thelledy asked, "Will you take an active part in this?"

"I will contact Faren Kiricky, and try to obtain by honest diplomacy what we have failed to get by force."

"And then?"

"And then we will attempt to deal with Demsing."

9

In the broadest sense of the word, technology and technique have the potential for becoming exercises in the studied avoidance of action and perception. That they do not is testimony to the strength of Will and Idea.

H. C., Atropine

In the darkness at the bottom of the shaft, Demsing wasted no time on extravagant emotions, although he was aware of those emotions, as it were, existing in a vague continuum in reserve. Now he concentrated on action, sitting perfectly still in the darkness.

He had underestimated two things: the strength of their response, and the skill that had gone into it. Probably Tudomany had pulled that box-over-the-shaft trick before, and somebody remembered it, and that was all there was to it. The gang who had invaded the box? Slugs, some local hoodlums, who had been given no information and who had been expected to be sacrificed whether necessary or not. How many had that book bomb killed? He had no way of knowing. He breathed deeply, slowly, savoring the rancid taste of damp air. And again. *It's time we ended this.*

But first things first. This was not a place of safety, a place to rest, or explore within, as Tudomany had suggested. If they could plan that well, then they should also be able to know he was waiting at the bottom of the shaft. And they would come, in the dark, in soft black clothing, moving in the silent ballet of sudden death. *It's time we ended this.*

Tudomany was no claim on him. Demsing knew the underworld as well as any surface person could expect to, and it was expected that she had old scores hidden away, old enemies. They knew that, too, and nothing would inhibit them with her, as it might with Chalmour. And what about Chalmour? *It's time we ended this.*

They would expect him to move laterally as he could, rising all the time, reaching, reacting. Demsing had made his life work doing the unexpected, the irrational, the unpredictable. He would go *down*, into the unexplored bowels of Teragon, as far down as down was, even out the other side if it could be done. He had been squatting on his haunches, but now he stood up to his full height and flexed his hands in the darkness. *I will go inside, whatever lies there: and for myself, the same, inside and negotiate with demons. And if I meet the Angel of Death, I will turn him loose to walk the surface with feet of fire.*

And there was something about that, too, which resonated like a tuning fork with something lost, just out of reach.

*   *   *

To advance, one first takes a step back. Then forward. To descend, one first goes up, because the little square pit at the bottom of the shaft was a dead end, and even if it had possessed the finest door on Teragon he would not have gone through it. He climbed up, quick and flowing like a cat moving against time, missing the firt cross-shaft the second, the third, even the fourth and fifth But the sixth, that was the one, and it was a long way up. Why the sixth? It had to be the sixth, the number rang in his head, six, six, six, six. Something he knew, but did not know why he knew. And they didn't. Six.

Six it was.

And sixth up was a good choice, because it opened up a little, good enough to be fast as a roach in, and then it began slanting down, down, down, in long swoops and runs, joining with others, intersecting, dropping, not a straight section in it. He used his nose, his ears, his proximity sense, touch, and only sometimes eyes, because sometimes there were small lights, enough to see a little by. He was terrified, truly terrified, more so than at any time he could ever remember, not of them who followed him but of what awaited him at the farthermost corner of the dark: himself, the concealed one, the one who remembered things which could not be, never had been. Down.

In a rare moment of lucidity when he stopped to catch his breath, Demsing noticed that there were lights. Not many. Most of them were burned out.

But there were some. More, in fact, as he went down.

He thought about it, and understood that he was lost. He welcomed it. He got to his feet, and began descending again. And as he went, he muttered to himself, to the dark, to the air that had begun to throb with the unseen and unknown hand of deep machinery, *Chalmour, Chalmour, hang on, I'm coming back . . . Something will come back.* And the way turned steeper. Now ramps and tunnels wouldn't do; the way became stairs and slides, and the slides were always lit at the bottom, dirty and dim fixtures, some of them out, but always some burning behind translucent windows. Who changed them in the upper levels?

There was one long slide, longer than all the others, and when he slid out into the chamber at the bottom of it, he saw before him, at the opposite end of the chamber, an open doorway into an open shaft, and there were no other exits. Two other slide-shafts, just like the one he had come down, entered the chamber. The slides down, an open hall, and an ogive-arch doorway into nothing.

Demsing walked slowly, approaching the portal with vertigo before he got to it, properly. Something in him knew what he was going to see. He looked over the edge, holding on to the side, which was not *Kamen*, but an inlaid design in various metals, their colors shifting in the uncertain light. Above, it was simple: a few meters up, the shaft ended in a dome, from whose underside protruded an odd decoration of multicolored metals like the inlay design of the portal. Some small spotlights shone, dim and red; others were burned out. Down, there was no end. There seemed to be a slight haze in the shaft, which was cylindrical in cross-section, which distorted the far distances. No matter. As far as he could see, the shaft had no end. And down there, the air was heavy. It was heavy here, and warm.

The soft thrumming of machinery was almost gone, and it was all above him. Down there, it was quiet. He looked around the receiving-chamber, looking for signs of passage. He found his way from the middle slide. Marks. There wasn't much dust. None elsewhere disturbed. Nobody came here. Nobody had ever been here. This was the place, then.

One place was as good as another, and he settled down near the portal, resting his back against the wall. It felt reassuringly solid, although he could feel a faint vibration in it, several frequencies overlapping, at the very limit of perception. He settled into himself, relaxing with that peculiar sense of duality of falling, drifting into sleep and waking up from thinking. Now. He waited, letting it come at its own pace, and as it did, he saw how he had always controlled it, pushing a little *here*, holding back *there*, stopping *here*. Not this time. There was something beyond, just as there was a bottom to the shaft behind him, and so he let it go as it would. It apparently had its own pace, too. Sometimes it almost stopped, and he remembered the image of a slow and looping river, worming across the flat surface of a delta, pouring out the suck and glut of a continent into a sea. There were no seas on Teragon, never had been, never could be. Not Teragon. No, not Teragon. At the sharper turns of his drift, he caught flickers of abrupt, broken mountains rising from the tumult of the sea in the dawn, a rich brown color, a black ocean, an impossible neon-indigo sky, time slower than you could measure, a sun drifting up impossibly slowly out of the distant ranges farther east. Gone. Yes. That was the right way, where it was deep down, where the images came fast and thick, too fast to identify individual segments. Here. Now.

There are things hidden within all of us which we write over because they do not fit the piece we have chosen. But we can only paper over them, not erase them. They live beyond us, they form our clothing, our sexual preferences, our speech (O traitorous instrument!) which conceals ideas thousands of years old, invented by leering filthy barbarians squatting by the greasy campfire, whose names we never knew, whose names we could never know, but whose horrid personas are resurrected in us, that flit from body to body, which are to *them* like shadows within which they may conceal themselves, and one fine day, at the crisis, all *our* fine talk goes out the window, thrown out the window and forgotten, *overforgotten*, never remembered, like the foil cover of a prophylactic in a moment of blind lust. Yes, lust. And at our finest hour, Zabbakak the Barbarian materializes in our hearts and extracts a few seconds from our lives.

The evil and the good and the neutral, also. The abilities and gifts we paper over because they cause sight we'd rather not have, inconveniences to the present. All those things. Demsing was no different there and he knew it. He had all those demons, and knew them by name. But there was more in him, and his names for *those* things were secret names he dared not whisper even in the dark of the back side of his mind. How he *saw*. What he used was only the echo of something greater. How he instinctively *knew* what motions to make in a fight, the inevitable flow of it. That, too, and the images of a past he'd never had, they were there, too. They were all manifestations of a single concept shining in the dark he had avoided, because "it didn't make sense." Of course it hadn't. It was only one, out of an entire universe of things that didn't fit, that avoided neat categorization, whose central ideas, whose basic principles walked among chaos and smiled and bestowed benedictions, but whose import was implacable.

He closed down his mind and walked among symbols of existence within himself. He saw that he could slow Time and perceive better the arrangement of the dance of the glowing parts, that seemed to shine in a dark cavern like golden wires. He had done this before. But only a little. Now he slowed it without stopping, and along one axis, the dance of the wires, the golden worms slowed, slowed, and drifted almost to virtual stop, and there he saw and comprehended that here was the complex symbol of his own identity. And as if along another dimensional line (which he did not try to understand, and in not-trying, saw more of it), there were more Demsings replicated in a line, one after another. He looked closer. No. Not more Demsings. More people. They were not his parents in the flesh: they were further back, different. The process of reproduction was a wall. These were him, continuity, and not-him. And their identities were different, alternating male-female. He moved closer, and manipulated the figure, one part of it, that replicated in all the figures, there were six of them and he was number six, (and there were more out the other side of Time, too, a procession extending into a shadowy infinity as hazy as the bottom of the shaft) and the fragile barrier he had built dissolved before the corrosive power of memory and he saw that they were him and he was they, and in the sudden flood he *knew* who he was and who he had been: Demsing Ngellathy. Nazarine Alea. Phaedrus. Damistofia Arart. Rael. That one. Tiresio Rael. And Jedily Tulilly, the rough clay they had started with. Jedily was just an empty shell, whose contents had been mined out by the others along the chain of personas, and he saw how it was done, the whole thing, how to initiate it, how to control it, what its tradeoffs were. Jedily-Rael-Damistofia-Phaedrus-Nazarine-Demsing, a light was growing inside him as the contents of those personas flowed into Demsing, last of the line and it peaked to a soundless explosion which whited-out everything, and when the radiance faded away, he knew he was the Morphodite, the changer, the immortal shapeshifter, the changer of worlds. He saw how he read the structure of the wave of the present, yes that was exactly what it was, a wave, moving among varied environments, and

there were other waves, too, and a medium for
them, and another higher-order world in which
such waves moved, unthinkable entities moved *there*
(not even as the Morphodite had he seen this before). And he saw the simple process by which one
controlled those waves, how one searched out and
found the key to Change, and moved that key. At
the base of every human expression of collective
organization, one person rested who defined that
thing, and that one person was not the chief, but
the bottom. They never knew it, nor did anyone
else. Unseen and unknown symbols of power, they
moved, serene in ignorance. Their real power in
the outside world of appearances was invisible,
while the seeming lords of the world of appearances were like little clanking windup toys that
crawled, scuttled, or rolled about like cheap little
toys. Some of them were nothing but apes with
big mouths, and dumb little plastic hands that
clashed cymbals. They were the least of the least,
prisoners of the collective, mere visible symbols of
it, powerless and willbereft. Every person. *Every*.
Each. Was dualistic—central definer of one thing,
slave of another. Humanity was a vast collective
network of these threads of causality. Go for the
outer symbol, the posturing chief, and you did
nothing: the organism could always grow another
head, and did. Assassinations were the fulmina-
tions of impotent fools, *Bonbinans in Vacuo*.

Rael was the first to use it. Demsing saw that.
But Rael had been required to use an elaborate
system of computation, cumbersome and Qabalistic.
He did not know it, but he was, had been, still

deeply in the shadow of Jedily, where they had started the Morphodite, and that elaborate system of computation had been her way. With each version, the process of visualizing and perceiving the Reality and how to manipulate it became more subtle, more abstract. By the time Nazarine had been reached, she did nothing but draw complex abstract ideograms on a piece of paper, and apply rules of Change to them. Like the *I Ching*, but more so. And for Demsing, six generations of The Morphodite now produced the result that he no longer needed outside symbols: he could do it entirely internally, within his mind's eye. Look, and Will it. That was all.

He set up the symbol for all that he had on Thelledy, Galitzyn, Chalmour, all of them, almost off-handedly, easily, tossing it to the change casually, reveling in his ability. And as quickly recoiled from the Answers though he had been stung, as though a mine had exploded in his face, a rifle butt in the teeth, a rubber hose in the night. He saw Chalmour outlined in radiance like a goddess, glowing threads flowing out of her all over Teragon, enveloping the planet like a golden web, and reaching beyond, into space, into Time. No wonder he had, in the world of appearances, moved to her, become her lover, instinctively. There was nothing like this anywhere in the combined memories of all the creatures the Morphodite had been. Nothing comparable to her. She was unique in Time, a unique nexus of expressions, and now for her to be harmed, injured, killed, or even moved out of her own course in any way, had consequences of such magnitude he had difficulty finding adequate expressions for it. *He* himself had a unique place in relation to her, but he could only move along a narrow path, even with his powers.

These things were never permanent. They constantly reformed, shifted, moved around. The mana passed on. And so, eventually, did Chalmour's mana, her reality as Talisman. Demsing *saw* the net of the Golden Web unraveling in its own way, the focal points and junctions reforming, shifting, the mana passing on. Chalmour would not always be thus, but throughout her life, she would always be a focal point, an intersection of lines of control.

He saw that the girl was a treasure beyond price, and that she was a key to the Wa'an School, that for now whatever happened to her was to happen to them. He could reach them through her, and Rael's old system of killing the foundation was crude and brutal beyond belief. But because of her interconnected linkages with all the other things she was, the golden web, he could not manipulate the Wa'an School through her without disastrous side effects elsewhere, incredible and explosive consequences. He saw in this why it was so, how they had connected their fate to hers, by the simple and arrogant acts of a few. The coupling in Reality mirrored the coupling which had taken place in the world of bodies. And as they had wounded her, so they had wounded themselves, and the whole order of which Chalmour was center shook and trembled. They sensed it, too. They were deep in the Art themselves, yes, you could approach this through the channel of the Martial Arts. Yes. The result was not as good as his way, not as clear an access to the Center, perception, and Control, but it went further than any other extant system. Demsing could even derive the Grandmaster's name. Telny. She couldn't see it as he did, but she could smell it, could hear the pounding of Destiny coming close with the careless acts of ... of ... Yes, his name was Ilyen, and of course, the amateurish hubris of Thelledy. He saw it.

Demsing saw it in the web of what was, in Reality. It was indefinite in some areas, clear in others. It had to be that way. He felt no jealousy, no envy, no sense of property. He felt only concern, for her, for what she was enduring, not the priceless release and gift of the self, the baring of the light that was in us all, but something that worked as a kind of rape, and in many ways was worse than rape, because it was irresponsible manipulation for the sake of the exercise of the power to manipulate, and in that was an echo of all the petty little assholes who had ever jerked someone around. Every tinhorn little straw boss, every desk lifer, every status-dingbat dipshit. And Demsing spoke clearly and ringingly in his private window into the eternity, *It's time we ended this.*

10

If you have to remind others of your authority, then functionally you don't have any—at least anything that will last while your back is turned.

H. C., Attitude Papers

When they did meet, it was under an atmosphere of considerable distrust, only partly alleviated by the admission of Telny, in candor, who she was and whom she represented. She had been required to go one step further, and conduct the meeting with Faren in an office under the ownership of the Water Cabal, with company guards nearby; that she had agreed to this protocol without any hesitation spoke well of time pressures and a bad situation somewhere else, and she had not seemed to care who had seen it. Certainly, to the sharpened senses of the average inhabitant of Teragon, such actions were statements of current conditions that spoke so plainly that the words that went along and rationalized such acts could effectively be ignored.

Faren sat across a low table from the younger woman; and Telny, for all her projection of competence and mature authority, was considerably younger than Faren. She was not intimidated by Telny: she had seen worse, traveling among the stars. Doubtless, Telny was both dangerous and powerful, but to offset that, she was also nothing more, or less, than a variety of local tough, and Faren was not impressed.

Telny said, in a low, slightly hoarse voice with no apparent accent or mannerism, "There are no recording devices?"

"None, as we agreed. They signed a penalty contract with me and lodged it with Klippisch's group, with interest provisions. As tight as the Water Cabal is, and as little as they pay, I regard that as something close to absolute security."

"That was also my assessment. Well, then, to the matter at hand. I will speak plainly and without tricks: we need information on Demsing, and we are willing to pay for it."

"Pay for it?"

"I quite understand that such a situation is analogous to the deplorable practice of paying for sex, when the ideal is that such communications should, in an ideal world, flow freely. But such is the case."

Faren looked away, and then back to Telny. "I have few needs and live a simple and a direct life. What I have is sufficient, as far as money goes. For a long time, Demsing helped in that, but I no longer need it. No money. But I would hear your reasons. That is real exchange, real money. Tell me."

Telny had expected difficulty, but not this kind. *Offworlders!* But she did not hesitate. That was why she, and not someone else, was Grandmaster. *Choose! Right or wrong, but choose!* She said, "Normally when we do surveillance on a person, as we come to know more about the target, a more complete picture emerges. We have done such work, directed at Demsing, but it seems that the reverse is true, and I am now in a difficult position of sensing with all my instincts that things are going wrong, deadly wrong, with an increased risk to myself and the organization of which I am a part. I need hard information before I can proceed."

This was the moment Faren had hoped would never come. For thirty-five standard years she had aged, hoping against hope that this would not be. She had done everything she could to prevent it. Now, what could she tell this "local thug," however self-assured she seemed to be. The universe was full of more fantastic things than this overurbanized planet could imagine, deadly things that made their roughhouse little world look like the bush leagues. Here, they murdered by night. There, they coldly and casually wrote whole planets off, entire ecosystems, erased not peoples, but entire cultural concepts. She knew this well. Nazarine had told her. And could this idiot understand what she was pressing for release? She doubted it.

She said, hesitantly, "Demsing has certain abilities which were hidden from him during the process of growing up. We arranged his life so he would not find them. Some of it he did find, but we had structured him so he would not go beyond imagining that he was just a little better than the ordinary. I spoke with him recently and saw signs that the wall was crumbling. Can you disengage from the situation you are in?"

Telny swallowed, and said, "Yes."

"Then you must do so, immediately, and compensate him, whatever you have to do."

"We are in danger?"

"Not just you. All of us."

Telny said, "We thought we were seeing some of this, but we do not know what we are facing. I cannot direct actions with no more justification than what I have. I believe you. But I need facts. You must reveal what you know, with the same sense of urgency we have, if what you say is all true."

"So you can hunt him all the better?"

"No. We want to negotiate with him directly. A group from Offworld hired us, not through me, to track him. As things have developed, it is becoming apparent that he may be a worse enemy than they. We know something of them, and what they can do. They have money (she said the word with some contempt), but they have little power, now. We have a dossier on Demsing, and the picture that is emerging is that up to now he has been operating at less than optimum, and at that, he equals the better of my field agents."

"At full awareness, which you may have triggered, you will never see the hand that smites you."

"An odd way of putting it."

"He can erase your organization from the face of

Teragon and you would never know how it happened and go down fighting phantoms out of your own collective imagination. That's the kind of power he has."

"That's a large claim, but I. . . ."

"I have seen him use it, and I have seen the hammer fall across the parsecs on a world neither he nor I ever set foot on. They owned a world; and they fell, nothing went right, a domino effect cascaded around them, and now they are scattered to the worlds. They will never have that power again, nor can anyone else in Time attempt what they did. That's how much power he has."

Telny said, after a moment, "I find that hard to believe."

"So do I. And there's something else about this ability: I think it steadily grows stronger and easier for him to use. That is why we tried to raise him so he would not know it."

"Wait. Demsing was a premature infant when you brought him onworld. We have the records. But you speak of him as if he was, before that. He does not know now, but he acted before. Unravel this."

"Demsing periodically is able to renew his identity by setting off a process of change within his own body. It takes about twenty standard years off his life, his apparent age, when he does it. His earliest identity is known, but his recollections of it are dim, worn out, and the early part of that was erased by the process which was used to create him."

Telny started to protest, but stopped.

Faren continued, "Demsing is potentially immortal. But not deathless: each change is like death. I knew him as his predecessor, and I raised him from infancy. She picked me because she trusted me, and I have carried it out. I failed to prevent what I swore to. We wanted the secret to die with him in this life. We did not know Teragon was such a hell. Instead, it has turned him into something unbelievably deadly. If you have made war on him, and lost track of him, even now it is possible he could be initiating Change, and when he finishes that, *he'll* be gone and you'll have to deal with *her*, and *she* will be the seventh identity that poor creature has inhabited in the last . . . about fifty standard years. Demsing is immortal but has died six times." It all tumbled out in a rush, as if words wouldn't contain it.

Telny exclaimed, "She?"

"It changes sex in Change. Each identity is different, and alternates sexual characteristics. Male. Female. It started as a female. Some lunatic research program to produce a perfect assassin. It escaped their control and destroyed their world, and then hunted its creators down and . . . eliminated any possibility that they could even think that again. I do not understand how it does it, but I have seen it work. Somehow, at full awareness, Demsing can *see* the unseen and unknown chain of microcausality that connects the parts of the universe, and with that sight, can find the weak link in your chain, and snap it. I knew Demsing as a young woman named Nazarine. She told me. Everything she could remember. At first, it was a killer. It killed the one unknown person who supported a world, an organization. But through each version, it learned, and has become more subtle.

Now? I don't even know what Demsing can do, and she who will come after . . . She will do things like . . . leave a water tap running. Move a trash can over a meter to the left. And everything will come unraveled, and you will never see her. I know. This time she will vanish."

"What are we looking for?"

"Demsing, if he hasn't changed. If he has . . . something like an adolescent girl, who might be anywhere from, say, fifteen standard, to maybe eighteen standard. I don't know what she would look like. He had only minimal control over the age rollback, and none over the identity. He doesn't know who he'll become. Only that it will be a girl."

"And she'll know everything he knows."

"Essentially. There is some memory loss in the process as well, but Nazarine had some control over what she lost." She stopped for a moment. "That's what I wanted to prevent. Change. If you've backed Demsing into some corner, and he calls up everything, and does Change, he'll have even more control, and she who is to be will have controls you can't imagine."

"Why are you telling me this?"

"Find him and contact him, promise him anything, but get him to hold off Change until he talks to me."

"What does it want?"

"To be ordinary. To be free of an unspeakable weight. There is no end to the process. Nazarine wanted to forget everything. She hoped going through infancy would erase most of it, and in its life to come, which was Demsing, it would never know, and someday die of old age. That can happen to it if it doesn't change. But she told me that each time, it gets further from being human. Its mind fills with the spectacle of the universe. It becomes a more unique creature. Eventually it will want others like itself, and will find the way to make more. Then it can reproduce. It can't, now."

"The report we have on Demsing states he is sterile."

"With humans. Not with one like him."

Telny looked down at the bare table. She said, "You knew nothing of Teragon, and you brought him here."

"We were looking for a stable life, some place sheltered. We knew it was a city, but not like it was. I lost him early...."

"Apparently we have lost him, too, and we may have given him powerful motivation to do the things you say he can do. To be candid, we took his girlfriend hostage. We hoped to contact him that way."

Faren looked across the table at Telny. "You couldn't know. But they have been killing its lovers and companions and sometimes its adopted children for generations of its life. Nazarine knew all of it."

Telny sat back, and asked, "How can I believe all this? There is nothing like this in any world I know of."

Faren felt her hands shaking. "You people are

the most adapted people I've ever seen, but you know almost nothing of the rest of the universe."

"We're not so back-country . . ."

Faren reached under the table, and produced a medallion, and handed it to Telny. It was silvery, heavy, and hard. Platinum. About a kilo of it. "Tell me what this object is."

She looked at it for a long time. "Exquisite workmanship, really nice stuff. I don't recognize it."

"In essence, it's a credit card, and in space, it's good all over the known universe. Bill it to the account of the Prince of Clisp, Planet Oerlikon. It was given to the fourth version by the Prince Emeritus. Take it and give it to Demsing, or whomever you find. It will remember it."

"Why do you have it?"

"Nazarine gave it to me in trust. Besides, it wouldn't spend here. I couldn't use it."

"They gave this to him?"

"Somebody trusted him. Nazarine told me, 'Phaedrus started an orphanage for refugee children, after a war.' "

"You believe that?"

"I believe she had it and used it. I believe things I saw her do. I believe it can Change. I was there. I saw Nazarine change into Demsing. She had been a friend, and when Nazarine ended, it was like something turned out a light. She was talking, and then nothing. It took a long time to turn into Demsing. There was a lot of body mass to get rid of. But I stayed there, through all of it. Awake. And I understand why it fears and hates Change. It is something much worse than death."

"We have a young woman, of about the right age . . ."

"Chalmour?"

"So she says, so we are told, so our reports say."

"I don't think so. Remember, it doesn't have control over who it becomes. That's something wholly under control of the process. It wouldn't do such a deception . . . I don't think."

Telny said, slowly, "If it's done a switch somehow, we've let it into the heart of our operation."

"Not possible. Too many coincidences, too shaky. Besides, I talked with Demsing not long ago. No, it's not Chalmour."

"You're sure?"

"Yes. But whatever Chalmour is, I advise you to treat her well. Demsing wanted her, permanently. There's that; and there is also the idea that he sees something in her we don't. She will be valuable to him. He will not permit another murder. And. . . ."

"Yes?"

"I just wanted to say I've never seen Chalmour. The last time I saw Demsing, he told me about her."

"How long does Change take?"

"The time is related directly to the change in body mass; the more it has to lose to reach the new state, the longer it takes. I think it needs at least a standard day to complete even close changes."

"Would Demsing have run a deception operation by you?"

"It's possible, but . . . I don't know. That entity, fully awake, tends to write all of us off once the hunt is up and, judging by the behavior I have seen, it's not entirely wrong to do so. If Demsing spotted you a while back, then he's had time to figure at least part of it out."

"One of our agents. . . . He spotted her some time back. Before Chalmour."

"You have the medallion. And turn Chalmour loose, if you're holding her. Has she been harmed?"

"Yes. No. I don't know."

Faren shook her head, slowly. "You can tell me what you want. That doesn't make any difference; Demsing knows, if he's reached for what he is. He knows." She paused a moment, and then added, "You have heard 'actions speak louder than words'? Very well. Actions leave physical traces, ripples in the fabric of time and space. That is what Demsing perceives. Actions and their echoes. Words, testimony, he knows all of us hedge the truth, lie, make excuses, rationalize, blame, anything to get the judge off our backs. He ignores words entirely and he will come to judge you according to what you did and what you intended and where you were careless and negligent. I have seen! Nazarine was gentle and full of light and love, but she was also implacable, relentless, she heard no pleas, she did know the meaning of mercy. Demsing with the ruthless values of Teragon may well be something beyond anything we could imagine, and if he's changed. . . . I must advise you that if you have harmed Chalmour, it would be best if you select a deity and subscribe your heart, because it now owns your fundament."

"Does it have a name, outside its identities?"

"The world where it was made . . . they called it The Angel of Death. The people who made it; they called it The Morphodite."

Telny nodded. "What sorts of capabilities does it have?"

"Assassin, terrorist, master of martial arts which haven't been invented yet, magician, so it seems to us, hypnotist, prestidigitator, student of occult paracausality . . . Nazarine did not seem to be operating at full power. And of course the ability to Change and vanish into the background. It can survive in minimal environments, blend into a background, use others for cover."

Telny stood up, as if suddenly galvanized by a decision. "So. I have decided. I must leave immediately. Like you, I have no recorders nor monitors. But I do have them outside, and I need to get this off right away."

"What will you do?"

"Release Chalmour, of course."

"That is a good place to start."

"Let us hope it is not too late."

"I am with you in that. If you find him as Demsing, send him to me. We may be able to annul the worst of it. He will listen to me, especially if he has activated. He will remember me as Demsing and Nazarine, both."

Telny nodded. "I hope that you are right. I will act on what you have given me, though it contradicts everything I have seen in my life."

Faren said, "Cynicism is a useful tool, but it serves poorly as a religion."

Telny nodded to indicate that she heard, but she

did not comment on Faren's remark. Turning away, she left the little office without looking back and made her way through the building, down stairs and through halls, as fast as she could, without running.

Outside, it was Primary-day. The shadows were alive with residents to Telny's practiced eye, and there were a lot of people in the streets, just like Gueldres was supposed to be. About a third of those visible were her own people, and more than half of those invisible were. She set out, reading the activation of the net of secret hand-signs as she walked into the net. It was full of urgency, rippling with potential, but she couldn't wait to shred those things out; in rapid succession she made the hand and gesture motions that would send forth her orders: *On pain of death, release Chalmour immediately, with her own clothing. No surveillance, repeat no surveillance. Put out the word through the net, all receivers, we request parley, will pay indemnities. Demsing to be received no traps no deception. Urgent. I Telny Lossoroch command.*

Around her, the flickering of the net of watchers took the message, reflected it, rolled it around and sent it onward, spreading in ripples out of her sight, to the ends of the world. Gods of Teragon! They'd have her sweeping the floor in a trainee's Chapter House after this. If she survived.

The net was still trembling, flickering, jumping like an interrogatee's smelly hide, still demanding her attention. She sent back, *Report on Galitzyn.*

The net quieted, became still, transparent, and

almost winked out of existence. In the silence of the signs that followed, Telny picked up one sender, who spoke for the net. *Galitzyn is gone. Vanished. Nobody saw anything.*

Telny felt a shiver run along her back, something she hadn't felt since she had been a girl in training. How long? Forty years ago? She kept on walking and sent back, *Comply with the order.* And she thought, *I had better alert the whole Order. This might be ugly.*

11

The shells which survive the surf, to lie on the beach for the collector to find, are of necessity the stoutest and the strongest; not so much the fragile, the subtle, or the evanescently beautiful; and the softer, more subtle little mollusks who secrete such shells are even more rarely seen.

And so it is with words: words clothe ideas very much after the fashion of mollusks and seashells, and in our lives as speakers, most commonly, only the industrial-strength words survive, save on the calmest coasts. With one, as with the other, it is foolish to imagine that what we have found is all that is, or that what we have found is most numerous, or most important to the environment of which it is part. Easy it is to understand this of shells and the sea, harder to see it true of words. And it is good to remember that in the sea, there are mollusks who have no shells (Nudibranchs), which correspond to ideas which have no words.

H. C., El Torre Quemado

Demsing still inhabited his private universe in the anteroom where the shafts converged, looking back to find examples of the actual manipulative use of the skill his abominable creators had given him. Seen in the curiously dualistic lifeline of The Morphodite: a personal recollection, as intimate and himself as much as a childhood memory from here on Teragon, and as close; and a vivid and accurate account of ancient history, eons back in time. He *was* Rael, and he wasn't.

Rael took forever to run his interminable calculations, but his results were fine-tuned and accurate. Demsing looked back to that with a strange kind of mingled awe and technical criticism, and at the Satan's Bargain that Rael had made with his creators, too. The next persona, Damistofia, had used the skill only to *see*, and had not used it fully as an instrument. True, she had defended herself, and she had killed, but that had been tactical defense and passion, and he saw within the system that when you released those drives, there was no result in the macrocosm. None at best, and there were counterproductive possibilities. Passion alone was almost always destructive to the self.

As for Phaedrus, there was a strange character whom Demsing did not entirely understand. What Phaedrus had done had been based on a desire to protect the innocent, and that was well-founded. People who would use terrorism against orphans just to insure they got him, and who used that as an opening statement, would not have hesitated at even deeper turpitude, would not even have blinked at it. Peccant souls! And sick, deeply sick. Why hadn't he looked for the door which would have opened the very jaws of Hell itself upon the perpetrators? Phaedrus had wanted peace deeply.

Nazarine had used it all, and used it well, and had not flinched from the necessity she had found at the end of her segment of the life they all shared. Yes. Kham, Cesar Kham had been the key person, the nobody-who-ruled his own system, and the correct action had been the Zero Option—do nothing whatsoever. But that situation, by the strange, strange logic of the system of analysis they all used, required a validation, an extra push, to become real and powered by Will, and the only sacrifice she had possessed had been herself, and she took it, unhesitatingly. And that with the knowledge that she might end the war with that. That it failed cast no darkness upon the aim she had voluntarily given up her identity for.

What were the courses open to him now?

It was something like the game of chess, with certain modifications: when attacked, one had four choices: to move the threatened piece out of danger, to interpose another piece between attacker and attacked, to attack the attacker by direct assault or by making the consequences of the intended attack too costly, and of course, to do nothing. But with this proviso: all situations are fluid and changing, and the pieces have values which follow no recognizable system. And one other: a decision was called for now and could not be put off, or much more serious things would begin to happen. A balance had been disturbed, and a large mass was now improperly supported.

Yes. Those were the demands of what he saw

before him, but there was another element to this, and that was Chalmour.

Chalmour was not the unseen base of any system, at no point in this symbolic plenum did she generate anything by being, as did others. But she connected things and articulated moments of inertia from one system into another, and another. She was a channel, a conduit, and this confronted Demsing and all the pasts who spoke through him with a situation for which his system of perception had no easy answers, or indeed, apparently no answers. He remembered, dimly, how the industrious Rael had come across this possibility when he had explored the boundaries of the field of perception and control, that such a type could exist, a linker, in the corporate systems the Morphodite perceived. Rael's description still rung in his head: stay away. There were equivalent nightmares lurking in the solution to the n-body problem in which n is greater than two, and in fact that was one of the avenues they had used to reach the state of being that was The Morphodite. This was the replicated version of that problem. But despite its complexity, there was one simplicity to the situation now which was easy to perceive, and that was that as far as he could see, there was no way to affect anything outside himself without the shock of the afterwave of the deed passing through the girl, damaging or distorting her beyond repair.

It was not a matter of "fault" and "blame." It was not "cause" and "effect." Those things were illusions the Reality covered its nudity with. She had not put herself in this configuration, and he had not put her there, and indeed, no one had "put" her there: that part of the wave which was Teragon had revealed itself so that she could be no other place, and he Demsing had helped along with all the rest.

He backed out, and re-entered again, beginning now to feel weariness from the continued strain of maintaining the distortion of subjective time necessary to perceive within the underworld inside himself. He knew with ordinary logic that he could only do a timeslip once, meet someone as one identity, go through two *changes*, and meet that person again, so *change* was not really open to him. But there was more to it now than that: *to change at any point even remotely near this point in Time would cost him Chalmour. All lines were blocked.* He could not use *change*, period.

He looked back into the shadows of the personae he had been; Nazarine had lived through such a knot, a place where one couldn't move, and had lived through it by simply waiting it out until the moment came. His grip and concentration began slipping. But he had to extract Chalmour out of the position she was in. And when he tensed the net for the Answer, it flexed instantly into an Answer he couldn't doubt, it came through so clearly: *Only Chalmour can free herself.*

Blocked every way. He let go, and began the long float back to consciousness, feeling drained and weak, worn and beaten. It could not be done, directly or indirectly. But he had seen something. Not much, but something. Galitzyn. He could approach Galitzyn-Vollbrecht, and around that nexus, he had a little more room.

Demsing opened his eyes, feeling the weight of his eyelids as an insurmountable downdrag, his entire body yearning for the hard floor. He was back. Nothing was changed: he was still in the place where the slide-tubes discharged into an anteroom of the glowing shaft into the depths. It was quiet, and the light was dim. He looked wearily into the open, curving mouths of the slide-tubes, all now going up. They were a way out, but not a good way, or an easy one. It would be neither pleasant nor timely to make his way back up those tubes.

Then it occurred to him how much he had missed, concentrating on the things his head had been full of. Demsing pinched himself, to keep awake, and to remind himself of his quite everyday stupidity: *the slideways all ended here, an anteroom, and then the shaft. The shaft had to be the only way out. And it had to have some way of controlling descent. Here was the place where the rapid transit began, into the interior.*

And there was something more. *This system of slide-tubes, shafts-down, and all of it could not have been made at any time by the humans who inhabited Teragon.* No one had questioned it, or, if they had, their question had been forgotten in the wash of Time. They had been busy, those early discoverers and colonists, and their descendants, and the immigrants, they had been even busier, and over Time, they simply looked the other way. He slowly got to his feet, forgetting for a moment the fatigue which dragged at him. This was not an end, here, not even a small one; but he could not see how much of a beginning it could be, but when, out of habit, he used his old shallowtrack system, the one he himself had learned to use, he could feel the echoes in it, of something greater than he could see from here. And one other thing: That the answer he was looking for, and the key sequence of acts he needed, lay farther on. The knot unraveled—there.

For a long time, or what seemed to be a long time, Demsing stood in the portal of the glowing shaft, looking down at the curdled, faded, indistinct bottom, somewhere out of sight. He went back over his suspicion again; this had to be a drop-shaft into a deeper region, and one that was fairly important, judging by the junction of the slideways. That it had to be, and at one time it would have had to have a means of slowing the descent. It wasn't wide enough for creatures with wings.

But at one time didn't mean, necessarily, now. The machinery could have been turned off, or, more likely, could have simply worn out. He considered the evidence of the small lamps along the way, how some of them were obviously burned out, or broken. All it would take would be one critical component in the braking system of the shaft, and the machinery would fail, and somewhere down there, a body would meet something more solid.

He turned back into the junction chamber and looked for something he could toss into the shaft, but there was apparently nothing, no loose stones, no trash, nothing he could throw. He moved slowly around the walls, looking closely, searching for a loose piece he could pry loose. It was there that he found something else which added to his suspicions: the surfacing of the junction chamber was not made of the concrete-like *Kamen*, but was something different. Harder, slicker, tile-like, but not with a shiny surface. He tapped at a section of the wall; it sounded solid, with a chinky surface sound that suggested something ceramic, or hard stone, and metal, all at the same time. There were no seams or signs of jointing. He hadn't noticed before, because he hadn't been looking for a difference. Everything was made of *Kamen*. But not this. It looked tough, and permanent. Whoever or whatever had made this chamber had intended it to last, and last it had.

Puzzled, he turned back to the portal, to see if there wasn't some clue there he had overlooked.

The walls of the shaft, as far as he could reach around the edge of the portal, seemed to be of the same substance as the walls of the chamber, which he reached by stepping on the inlaid metallic lintel and reaching as far as he could. Disappointed, he stepped back from the edge, and as he did, he heard a low vibration start up from somewhere far below, barely audible, a humming at the very edge of perception, and overhead, the domed roof of the drop-shaft made a sudden, sharp, clicking noise, actually low in volume, but in the stillness, it sounded loud as a shot. There was no echo.

It could not be the wall, or the surface. But it could be the lintel. He stepped on the inlay again, with all his weight, and nothing happened, but when he removed his foot, the same thing happened again. A low vibration starting up and fading, from far below, and a more substantial movement from above, in the dome. The lintel was the activating switch. You stepped on it, and off into the shaft, and that activated the machinery. Both steps, and with the thrust out into the shaft. He took a deep breath, blanked his mind, stepped on the lintel, and off into the shaft, avoiding thinking, except the consideration that if he was wrong, it would end fast at the bottom of the shaft, wherever that was.

He wasn't wrong. As he stepped off, the hum at the bottom quickly ascended into a soft, whining hum of power, and the dome opened up like the petals of a flower, upwards, too quickly for him to see the movement, and his descent was slowed by a surge of air rushing up the shaft. It still worked.

At first, he tumbled violently and dropped faster than he liked, but as he fell, Demsing was gradually able to stabilize himself and control his rate of descent a bit better. He was facing downward into the wind, and could not look back up for long without disturbing his equilibrium, but he watched the walls and managed to find a midpoint where he was reasonably stable and falling controllably fast. Now he was going somewhere.

The shaft was longer than he had imagined it to be; buoyed by the flowing air in the shaft, Demsing fell for what he considered to be a long time, and the humming noise did not get appreciably louder as he fell. The wind around him whipped and tore at him, his face, ears, hands. Whoever had originally designed this mode of travel either did not mind such abrasion, or had some way of avoiding it. Demsing fell on. He felt about carefully for a position which would allow him greater speed, and moved into it, feeling the wind increase.

For a moment, he heard the humming adjust itself to a different rhythm, and with his heart pounding in sudden fear, he felt his speed increase. Damn! It was tracking him somehow, and had decided to give him more speed. Once it reached a steady level, the sense of change stopped, the air flow stabilized, and Demsing fell into the bowels of Teragon, slightly headfirst, the bottom of the shaft still dim and indistinct, hidden behind a veil of thickened atmosphere.

How far did he fall? Demsing had no way of knowing, because his speed of descent was unknown. The nearly featureless walls of the shaft gave no clue, and what light there was seemed to emanate from the walls themselves, an endless cylinder down down down down. By his chronometer, he fell for three hours and more, without a break. Something, he thought between seventy and a hundred kilometers, maybe more. The air was thick and pasty to the touch, and warmer.

Signs that the fall was coming to an end began to appear. He went through a zone in the shaft where the lighting changed from a steady glow to a weak alternation of brighter and dimmer parts, which he sensed as a patterned, regular flickering as he fell past the zone. He opened up a little and slowed himself, and heard the hum increase, to put more air out. There was another clear, featureless section, and then another patterned section, this one different from the first. He still could not make out any structure to the bottom, although he could now see that there was one, a darkness at the far end of the shaft. He felt light-headed and hallucinated; perhaps he should do nothing. The shaft seemed both automatic and responsive. But he opened up to the maximum drag, and after a moment, felt the shaft respond with even more wind. He was definitely slowing, and the bottom was clearly approaching, coming closer, still featureless, and the wind was building to a roar.

The bottom of the shaft was a grating, made of the same material as the walls, which glowed as he approached it, slower than he thought he had been moving, and when his weight touched it, the humming, still sourceless, dropped off abruptly and the air stilled. The shaft was empty, silent, and the silence was louder than the roar of wind had been. He had landed on all fours, and for a long time, he lay on the grating, breathing an atmosphere which seemed liquid and dense. It was distinctly uncomfortable, but for the moment, he thought he could bear it, because wherever he was, he was undeniably there. He had arrived.

12

If one performs a questionable act of bad
faith, deception, general wickedness, selfishness
or destructive revenge, and then justifies that
act by citing some philosophy of Good Intent,
what happens instantly is not that by some sort
of spurious magic one makes an evil act in the
bottom-line real world good, but that one con-
taminates the philosophy and renders it spurious by one's contemptible use of it. Individually,
such acts counted one at a time seem to make
little difference, but a lot of them add up, and
can in time turn a thing once invented as a good
into a powerful instrument of consummate and
devouring evil.

H. C., Atropine

Ilyen came no more to Chalmour's cell, a fact
which both relieved her and frightened her: the
former from direct response, the latter because she
wondered, *and after that performance, what other
fun and games do they have up their sleeves?* Somebody who was far down in the hierarchy brought
her meals, and they did not make small talk when
they did. She had time to study this from several

sides, indeed she had plenty of time, but since no further interrogations or treatments occurred, she concluded that somewhere, off where somebody made decisions, something had changed about herself in relation to her captors. Something. But what? Very obviously they now had a problem, which she saw immediately: she knew that the Wa'an School had had a long-term interest in Demsing, and that, from little hints she had caught, Thelledy was almost proven to be involved in it from the beginning. At the least, it was suspected. They could, then, expect her to inform various people, Demsing and Klippisch for starters, and from that, inconveniences would certainly result. That was not a cheerful deduction.

On the other hand, the treatment she was now getting argued for something else, quite to the contrary: somehow she had become valuable to them. There had been a shift in values.

There were aspects of this that angered her, and she cultivated that anger. All the responses they had made to her were in relation to somewhere, someone else, not herself, and that was demeaning and degrading. That was the worst part of being a hostage, not any specific treatment, but for the nothingness it implied. That was not how she saw herself, nor had it been the way Demsing had acted toward her. There had been no break between his acts and his words. He made no expectations, required no demands, apparently valued her as she was, although she suspected he saw things in her she could not see herself. No matter, that.

So she examined the possibilities that seemed

open to happen to her, and how she might react to them, to increase the price they paid, so that they would understand the most valuable thing she had learned from Demsing: that every person, because each was unique, possessed a unique value, a potential, which made everyone a star, and that no one could be written off. No one.

So it came that she was surprised by what did happen: with no preliminary hints, the flunky who had been bringing her meals appeared with her old clothes, and wordlessly departed, rather pointedly leaving the door unlocked.

She didn't rush. Chalmour took her own time dressing, and when she was ready, she made one last inspection of the room they had held her in. It was empty of anything that was her, her identity. And as she stepped out into the empty corridor, she thought *And so they turn me loose, and even in that they contrive to remind me of what a nothing I am to them, just a tool. They have no more use for me, so I can go. We'll see about that, too.*

Not far off, the corridor deadended, on the left, so to the right was the only way out, and she set off without hesitating. It was an old corridor, because it went through several odd little jags and jogs off in odd directions, as if it had been adapted from sections of older buildings. There was still a sense of being underground, though, and from that she knew she had to find some passage going up. She was not worried about where she came out. They had not moved her long enough to get very far from Gueldres, and she knew her way around.

She found an ancient elevator, which worked,

and she stepped into it without hesitating, and pressed the up button, and ascended, and there were no surprises at the top, either. The door opened promptly.

She was in a plain foyer of a building which opened directly on the surface. She could see a street through the front windows. The foyer was finished off with a surface glaze which suggested somewhere in Ctameron, and she was pleased at that: *At least I won't have to fight my way out of Petroniu.*

A single figure stood by the door, backlit and silhouetted by the lighting from the street beyond. The foyer was lit, but not enough. At first, the figure was still, and Chalmour could not make much of an identification, but as she approached the entry, the figure moved, and she saw that it was a woman. An older woman, with careful movements, smooth and dancelike.

This is one of them, too. And her heart sank, but the woman made no move to stop her, or stand in her way. However, as she reached for the pushbar of the door, the woman spoke.

"We don't make many apologies, but this has to be one of them. I am Telny. I ordered this, and my response was in error. An imbalance has been created."

A thousand words eddied within Chalmour's mind, and she found it difficult to choose among them. Finally, hand still on the bar, she managed to get out, "That is understated. In what areas do you imagine such an imbalance?"

"We have inconvenienced you, stolen time which cannot be replaced. Restitution will be made."

With rare restraint, Chalmour said, "I am nobody, but I can easily see that you do not see the real problem. That alone will suffice for me." She surprised herself with the venom in her voice.

Telny's face remained blank. She said, "Nevertheless, according to our statutes and canons, there must be compensation made. Where shall we forward such compensation?"

Chalmour pushed open the door. "Send it to me, in care of Demsing Ngellathy."

"Do you know where he is? We would like very much to arrange a truce." The voice was quiet, controlled, and slightly sad.

Again, thoughts and incomplete retorts swirled in her mind, all of them unsuitable to her purpose, which was to injure, to damage. In the end, she thought nothing and silence might be the best of all. Chalmour walked through the door onto the street outside, and set off in a random direction, never looking back. She did not hurry, but walked purposefully, and after a while, was able to figure out where she was, somewhere in Ctameron on the side toward the Palterie. She assumed she was being followed and further assumed that they could do so without her being aware of it. Nevertheless, she first laid out a decoy course to make it appear she was headed toward her parents' neighborhood, and then altered course to bring her back into Desimetre, to Klippisch's place.

*　　*　　*

When she reached her destination, Klippisch was in, and pacing up and down in her office, declaiming to an audience of Dossifey and a couple of terrified apprentices. It was a major operation to slow her down. She had reason to be excited: two apprenticemasters gone, and the Mind vanished as well. At the first, Chalmour presented an obvious target, but with some prodding from Dossifey, at last Klippisch slowed down and began listening to Chalmour's tale. There was a lot that Chalmour didn't know, but she described Demsing's suspicions, his acts, and the responses which she knew had occurred. From these pieces, she could build a convincing argument that the disappearance of Thelledy and Galitzyn were connected in high probability.

At last, Klippisch stopped ranting entirely and sat down behind her creaking desk, and remained silent for a considerable time. At last, with a fist propping her head up by the jowl, she growled, "And so where is Demsing now?"

"I don't know. We were below Gueldres, about ten levels down, when we met Tudomany. Then there was the shaft. When they took me, it seemed as if I had gone down a long way, longer than ten levels. I do not know how far that shaft went farther down. I think they were expecting him to come back up, but he didn't."

Klippisch now faced the desk and put both fists on her cheeks, grumbling, "We don't know much about those lower levels. People don't go down there, never have. Would you? There seems to be no end to it, and although it's always been there,

there has always been the idea that no one could afford idle curiosity. We found enough room on the surface, and in the upper parts of the underground, to do the things we needed to do—the water extraction plants, the hydroponic compounds, the recyclers. Plenty of room. Too much, even. Almost another planet down there in surface area. And of course people have gone down there and never come back, too. No explanation, no remains, no nothing: just silence. So people stay out. And obviously those people who took you, they knew something about where to go."

"Yes. They knew that part well, but I had the idea that their knowledge was limited, too, that they had gone deeper than most, but not as deep as they could have. Demsing vanishing seemed to mystify them. It was not what they expected."

"I don't know how he's doing it without food and water, if he's looking for a place to hide; but Demsing always was good at doing without in a pinch, so he has longer than most people. Even so, after a while we will have to assume the worst. After all, anybody can have an accident."

"What about Galitzyn?"

"We're out looking for him. Him I'll have over a slow fire! He ran, the rat, but we'll find him, never fear. As for Thelledy, you won't see her again. She's halfway to the other side of Teragon by now—and that Ilyen, too. Sorry you had to put up with that."

"I should have paid more attention to Thelledy's lessons."

"You'd have had to spend a lot more time than

you had to stand off something like that; it takes years to learn to override your deepest instincts as they do, and believe me you got off light in that, too. They could have done a lot worse."

"I thought that at the time, but I did not know how far they could go. I don't, now."

"You don't normally see that particular use of skill directed toward females; usually it's used by girls against men, but it doesn't surprise me that they had someone proficient around. Their operatives would have to have something to work against to keep their skill level high, honed. That's a sport you can't practice alone, ha, ha!"

"I want to go looking for Demsing; will you lend me a couple of apprentices?"

Klippisch stopped short and focused on the girl's face. "That would be very foolish, Chalmour. You know where to start, but you don't know where he went, or why, or what might be down there. Under normal conditions, and even under most ordinary emergencies, I don't allow my people any farther down than fifteenth level or equivalent. Besides, they might be down there looking for him as well, and there you'd come with a gaggle of apprentices. . . . Besides, how are you going to track him through those tunnels? I'm telling you it's difficult even for the best trackers, and they know their maximum limitations and hold back."

Chalmour's face was still, but Klippisch knew the girl was deliberately holding it that way. She added, in a softer voice, "Listen. I know how you feel—you must do this. But believe somebody that was good to you: you go down there below the parts we know and that's two of you I've lost."

Chalmour said, in a low tone, resigned, "I'm of no value to you. I was scooped up like a sack of trash, locked up, fed and well-laid at will. Moreover, I didn't escape; they knew how valueless I was and tossed me out when they had done with me. Such a person needs more modest employment than agenting for Klippisch's Group."

"Stop! I'll not have that sort of talk! Not a word They turned you loose because your value had become a weight they could not bear. They do not ever *let* anyone go. If that had been their intent, they would have had you crawling around on your hands and knees, drooling and grunting and begging for more. And mind, *if* they had found your genetic patterns suitable, they might have made you a breeder, in some underground place they keep for themselves. Don't flinch! There are far uglier aspects of this than mere violence. There are places on this world where corruption runs deep and long in Time, and that Wa'an School is one of them. We know a little about them, but I am certain that what we know isn't even the half of it—or half of a half."

She continued, "And as for your value to me, you have become very valuable indeed, because you have survived what you have. Not many could have walked out of there. I know this because not many do. I was taken once, and I know what they can do. I was ransomed out, and for a year afterwards I had to fight myself to keep from wanting to go back. Do you understand? I wanted to go back. I didn't care. At least you saved enough to hate."

"I have to find him because. . . ."

"Because you think that what was saved was something Demsing called out of you, or perhaps put in you?"

It was a rude question, rudely put, and it struck home. Chalmour colored suddenly, her neck and face turning ruddy.

Klippisch said, "I'm accounted good at what I do. And what is that? Running a busload of terrorists? Managing and selling spies and assassins? Wrong, wrong, wrong! What I do is find the best in the human material that sifts through my small grasp, and putting it to the best use. Profit we need and profit we get, but not at the price of throwing out the best we find, or neglecting things that are not apparent on the surface. I want people with self-control, I want people who don't make crummy excuses for behavior that can't be called anything but bad from the ground up, and I damn sure don't want system-riders who con their positions with a hard sell with nothing behind it. This world, like all the rest, is full of those kinds of people, full to the brim. Do you believe me?"

"Yes. I believe that."

"Very well. Then believe me when I say that Demsing is the only person I know who is more fanatic on this subject than I am. Yes, he takes risks, and yes, indeed, when the time comes to be ruthless he is cold as ice. But it's always precisely what has to be done, like surgery, and no more. Whatever happened between you and him hap-

pened because what you *are* is intrinsically valuable, even if you can't see it. Do not be taken in by
the low estimation of you by criminals, nor over-
whelmed by an imagined influence of others. Steer
the middle course, and be your own person, your
own woman. That you are an apprentice here is a
measure of what I could see in you, what I saw in
you when we took you in. And the same with him.
If it was right, if it is still right, go with it and
don't look back."

"If he gets back."

"Yes. If he gets back. That, too."

"How do you know this?"

Klippisch leaned back in her chair, and put her
hands behind her head, flexing her sturdy arms.
"All of us who have survived are not necessarily
old fudds who practice creative obnoxiousness and
mutter about the good old days. These are the
good old days! Right now, and to the underground
of Teragon with the rest of it!"

"Well. . . ."

"Besides, I've got work for you. I have Dossifey
out looking for Galitzyn." Chalmour looked around
the office and suddenly discovered that the room
was empty of everyone except herself and Klippisch.
"And I've got to be out looking for a new Archive. I
need you here, to keep everything connected. There
are some operations going on, but they mostly
take care of themselves, and they don't need
moment-to-moment overseeing. Will you mind the
store while I'm out?"

"You'd assign that to an apprentice?"

"You're not an apprentice anymore."

Klippisch knew Chalmour was wavering, probably was settled into it, but she added, "And Demsing; if he can get back, he will. And if he can't, you can't save him. It has to be like that."

"And would he still want me, then?" It was a last resistance, and a last fear, at the very bottom.

Klippisch stood up and looked around to be sure no one was listening. She said, slowly, "Jealousy is the result of insecurity. He does not think that way. There are not many like him. Those kind of men . . . I'll tell you: With those, you can be yourself as you will without fear. That's good. But the price is that they don't accept less than the best, either. But all in all, that's what I'd take a chance on."

Chalmour stood up, and shook herself, like an animal getting over a chill, or perhaps a bad dream, or a sudden pain. "When do I go to work?"

Klippisch nodded and rubbed her hands together. "Now. Come around to this side. I'll call in. Give me your hand." Chalmour extended her hand and Klippisch took it, and, concealing their hands, rapidly spelled out numbers in the hand code to the girl. "You have them?"

"Yes."

"The first one's mine, and the second Dossifey. We both call in often, when we're in this kind of operation. And the third one is yours. These periods are short. But Dossifey should be calling in anytime, now. It's all yours."

"You knew I'd do this. . . ."

"It's the best way. And don't worry. Stay on your feet and don't fall, now. You've made it past the worst part."

13

We imagine that the entire issue of any work of art in any medium lies in the beginning, in the creation. All our mythology supports this, reinforces it. But the real problem, which separates art from artifice, is in knowing when to stop.

H. C., Atropine

Demsing examined the bottom of the shaft carefully, everything he could perceive. The air was dense, heavy, sluggish, and hard to breathe. The sides of the shaft were identical to the top. The same material. Whatever, it glowed weakly, but seemed to give off no heat. And in the side of the shaft there was a door, with a metal lever recessed in a streamlined depression. There was nothing that looked like a lock, or any device to prevent entry, so he reached for it, grasped it and turned the lever down, the way it seemed to be intended to move. The lever grated a little inside, but it moved easily enough, and with a push of medium strength, the door swung open.

Into a small room perhaps two body-lengths

across, square in plan. Demsing stepped inside and released the door, which closed on its own, latching as it touched. On the opposite side was a door identical to the first. Here, only the ceiling glowed. The room was absolutely plain, without decoration or symbols. He tried the door he had just come through. The handle pivoted down, but felt as if it stopped, momentarily, at a rest or a detent which held it for a moment. Then it released, he pulled it open, and looked out into the shaft and the grating floor. He released it and let it close.

Something about the way it closed and latched: it was not just a door, a security door to bar entry, but something more substantial. It sounded solid, even after all the time ... He had no idea how long this had been down here. It sealed. He turned to the other door on the far side of the little room, and depressed the lever, and it stopped at a point about halfway down.

At first, nothing happened. There was no sound. But soon Demsing's ears popped as air pressure equalized. The feeling of pressure continued, and his ears popped again, and again. The sensation of breathing syrup lessened, slowly. Here his memories from his other lives did not help him much, but he concluded finally that the antechamber was an airlock. Presumably, beyond this chamber, the air pressure would be similar to the surface.

What surprised him was the soundlessness of the process. He expected to hear machinery, pumps, fans, motors. There was none of this: the air pressure continued to drop, accompanied by the frequent popping of his ears, in total silence. And finally, after what seemed a long time, the handle slipped to its stop position, and the door swung inwards, with only the faintest of sound from its bearings.

A well-lit corridor led off into the distance. Here, all the lighting still worked, although some of the fixtures along the walls were slightly dimmer than the others. *How long?* The air had an odor, but it was very faint, and bore no identity he could recognize. It was neither stale nor musty, but felt fresh and recirculated. The odor suggested . . . machinery, perhaps. Walls, doors, things. He stepped into the hallway, wary as an animal, but there was utter silence. The hall arrowed off into the vanishing point of infinity. Far, far down its impossible length there was a suggestion of something, some detail he could not resolve, but nearby, the hallway was featureless and perfect. And clean.

Demsing was hungry, but he had ignored the pangs for some time. However, he was also becoming very thirsty, and that he could not ignore indefinitely. The fall down the shaft had, in addition to everything else, dehydrated him severely. He hesitated, thinking, *Suppose there's no water down there?* But he set out, not at a run, but with the long stride of a strong walk. There was no water where he was, and no way back up the shaft, unless it could also contrive to blow one back up that distance. He doubted it. And even if it did work in reverse, there was no water there, either. So it had to be forward.

Demsing walked on, but he felt like a burglar

who was a long way out of his depth. He had no idea what this enigmatic structure was, had been, could be. *But whatever it was, it had been built to last, and it hadn't been built yesterday, either. It was old; more than old. Ancient.* He could find no mention of this in the myriad things he knew about Teragon. Nothing. It was, in all probability, antecedent to the human settlement of Teragon. There was something else that nagged at him, too: the scale was different, in subtle ways which were not immediately apparent. It seemed, from the size of the shaft, the doors, and the hallway, that the builders were slightly larger than human-size.

Whoever had built it had strange ideas about distances—the shaft, with its impossible long fall, and then the hall, as featureless as the shaft. He walked with a stride that could cover kilometers, but the hall did not change, nor did the end seem any closer. There was only silence, and the lighted hallway. His footsteps resounded normally, but there was no echo, or reverberation. After a time, he fell into the rhythm of walking and forgot about staying alert in the present. He let it take him. And a lot of time passed.

Something began to emerge out of the hallucinatory distance of the hallway, but for a long time he paid no attention to it. He was becoming a little light-headed, and imagined that it would probably amount to nothing more than some sign, which would say something like: NO SMOKING.

It proved not to be a sign, but the first of a series of side portals into other regions. There appeared to be no order in their placement, left, right, large, small. There were no doors. Just openings, which seemed to pass through a maze or baffle. The first one was on the right, and proved to be, miraculously, a kind of sanitary facility. Or at least, so he thought. There were drains in the floor along the wall, and receptacles on the other side, with paddle-shaped levers. He tried one, out of curiosity, and the outlet produced a stream of clear liquid. Water? He smelled it, tasted it, gingerly. Water.

It made some sense. That room was the last before the long walk to the shaft. And again, that nagging sense of scale. The fountain had been higher than a human would have placed it. Well. They breathed air, and they used hydrogen oxide. It had tasted absolutely pure, with no flavor whatsoever, no hint of anything in it. Demsing drank as much as he could hold; he had no idea where he might find more.

Returning to the hallway, he tried the next opening. This one led to a blind cul-de-sac which seemed to have no purpose at all. Just an empty room.

The third opening gave way to a short corridor, and in this one the sound seemed a little close. The corridor ended in a T-junction, with a passage to the right and the left, with no signs. He looked down both. The alternate passages also ended in T-junctions. Momentarily stopped, Demsing made brief trips into each of the four possibilities, and looked down them in turn. Each one appeared to turn into ramps which went up or down at what he considered a fairly steep angle. A Maze? In all of them but one, the sound of his passage had a dead, dulled quality. This was subtle, and hard to prove, but one of the ramps up seemed to have more of a feel for space. Right, then left. He walked up the ramp cautiously, listening. The sense of space increased, but whatever the ramp led to, it was concealed behind several turns and landings. The turns were never curved, but had hard edges. At last, after ascending what seemed to him to a position higher than the main hallway, he saw the ramp ahead of him going up into an open space.

He heard no sound, no sense of presence, but Demsing kept to the edge of the ramp as long as he could, risking a glance, but he could not see anything. Whatever this place was, it was lighted in the lower parts, but dimmer above. He could not make out a ceiling, although he could sense one was there. He stood up and walked into it.

For a moment, nothing seemed to register, except the size of the hall. To his left, ramps led up into a slanted area that seemed to rise to impossible distances. But there were no seats or benches. Just oval depressions in the floor at regular intervals. On the right, the entire wall was translucent and glowed with the same light as the dropshaft. Below it, dwarfed by comparison, a bank of consoles stretched across the titan length of the room, along a slightly raised dais, which also had the oval depressions, but only along the edge facing the room. It had the look of an auditorium or a concert hall, or perhaps a council chamber. He walked gingerly up onto the dais.

There was no creature of any sort in this enormous room, whose size eclipsed anything Demsing could remember. The part of his memory he labeled "Nazarine" suggested that it might be as large or larger than some of the environment halls on major spaceships, several cubic kilometers at least. Whoever they were, or where they were, they liked things *big*. They lived underground, but they liked a lot of space.

There was no odor, so sense of presense, no trash, no dust. Everything seemed to have been left just moments ago, but the sense of long emptiness was like that of a tomb.

He approached one of the consoles, and looked at it closely. There were no read-out devices on the consoles. Just banks of what seemed to be oversize beige marbles, perhaps about three or four centimeters across, in recessed receptacles. Some of the consoles had similar arrangements of the little balls, others, different arrays. The consoles which had different arrays had less of them. But nothing anywhere which seemed to function as an indicator. No lights, no meters, no bar graphs, and no space where a screen might be formed.

He wanted to touch the console, if nothing more than to assure himself of its reality, but he held back, half-fearing that they might still be active, like the shaft and the airlock. There was no legend, no symbols. Whoever had once operated these consoles, to whatever purpose, had known what each little ball did. On the other hand, given the impression of overwhelming antiquity, he found it hard to believe that the consoles would still function. Machinery he could believe, but here was something more fragile.

And what had been the purpose of this hall? He

doubted that it had been an operational control room. The enormous space for audience seemed to belie that; one would not, he reasoned, conduct operational actions before a large audience, or could he make that assumption? This was something beyond his experience as Demsing.

Demsing called upon his memories from his other selves, shadowy figures which were undeniably himself, but also had, even now, phantom identities of their own. Nazarine, Phaedrus, those two were still fairly clear and distinct. Damistofia was weak and poorly defined. She hadn't lived long enough to stabilize as a unified personality. Rael was there, but only as abstracts. That personality could speak, but its voice was almost gone.

The only one of them who had knowledge of complex machinery was Nazarine, and her knowledge was second-hand, data she had obtained from a teaching program. She knew it, it was fact, but there was no hands-on experience to give it depth. The only thing she contributed was that somewhere on the console there should be either a switch to turn it on and off, or another to activate it, should it be on all the time.

None of them had any experience with aliens who used machines. Nazarine remembered things like gracile dogs, and Phaedrus remembered Bosels, whose intelligence was questionable. They could not help him!

He fell back on the computational system of the Morphodite: Zero. There was no matrix of actions and numbers of people to work with. There was nothing here to work with. Only himself. He would have to disturb this continuum to read anything from it, and without knowledgeable participants, he was casting in the dark.

Stuck.

Demsing shook his head. Not so! When gifts gave out, one still had oneself. Assumption: this is an auditorium. Conclusion: the consoles control displays of information, or entertainment. There are no read-outs at the positions: Conclusion: that the wall is the read-out. He looked closely at the consoles, and began to see an order to it. The consoles with fewer controls had the same number of banks as they had fully configured consoles on either side of them. It would take a crew to operate this thing to its full potential.

He touched one of the consoles. Solid and firm. The balls seemed to be in no special arrangement. Start somewhere. He touched one, felt it. What did it do? It rolled, and surprisingly smoothly, with an oily, dampened motion to it, despite the fact that it was dry. A linkage deeper inside? That one did nothing. Another. The same. Nothing. Demsing started going to each one, moving it in turn, fully expecting what he found, that the equipment was dead and still, even though the mechanical part still functioned. Nothing.

The last ball on the lower right only moved one way, horizontally, left-right. To left did nothing, but to right had an immediate effect: above, on the wall, a large hexagonal area brightened. And now the ball moved up and down as well. Up produced a stream of symbols flowing across the bottom of the illuminated panel, constantly changing, urging someone long forgotten to inconceivable actions and responses. The string of symbols moved very fast, but even if they had been still, they would have made no sense to Demsing. He could not determine if they were numbers or letters, or that such a distinction existed in that language. Demsing rotated the ball to the left, to turn it off, as he thought proper.

It did not turn off, but went dark, darker than its surrounding hexagons, and inside the dark field were random points and diffuse curdled smears, each one with a legend beside it, in the same characters as had been in the stream.

Apparently, the ball had to be moved in a certain order. He rotated it again, right, down, then left. The dark display winked out. Rapidly, he went through the same start sequence again, and the same dark presentation appeared. Demsing looked at it for a time, and then rapidly, he ran down the line of consoles, finding the activation ball-switch, and using the same prodecure, turned all of them on, and it was as he suspected, and the wall filled in with the dark display as he turned each one on. A picture filled in across the wall.

He looked up at it, but he was too close, and the display wall at this distance and angle conveyed no intelligence to him, so he moved farther out, into the gallery, onto the ramp and the implied seats, until he could see it more as a whole.

In a way, it resembled the night sky; points of light on a dark field would describe it. But this resembled no night sky with which he was familiar, and contained objects whose import was not immediately apparent. He was further hampered by the fact that on Teragon few people were interested in the stars and fewer still studied them, so that he actually knew very little about astronomy, or astrophysics. Essentially, the field before him displayed a large mass of stars, surrounded by smaller groups of them, and some individual points by themselves. By each group and by some of the individuals, there was a string of symbols, presumably an identifying tag of some kind.

The large mass, slightly to left center, was itself divided up into different parts. The outer parts were coded in orange, and formed a sphere which surrounded the central parts. The orange part extended out quite far, including several of the outer groups. Deeper inside, there was a blue disk, with recognizable ripples corrugating its surface, clearly a spiral feature. The disk was like a wheel, and faded out in the center. Inside the disk was another wheel in yellow with a conspicuous bulged center, and at the very center, one black spot.

Demsing opened up his memory and reached back for earlier personas, to see if this made sense to them. It did. Nazarine recognized it, and so did Rael, but Nazarine spoke for both of them, a condensation.

You're looking at a projection of the galaxy. Our galaxy. When you look up at the sky at night, the stars you see with the naked eye are all inside that. Then followed a swift image of basic astronomy, recalled and told simultaneously. Demsing was embarrassed to reveal to his former personas how provincial he had become in Teragon.

The little furry spheres are globular clusters. That number seems higher than I recall, but these folk may have better instruments. The larger patches are the irregular satellite galaxies. The two large ones, close in, are the Magellanic Clouds, which are not satellites of the main galaxy, but independent members of the Local Group, which have just made a close open orbit around the galaxy, their closest approach being almost directly over the galactic South Pole. Their suspected orbit is now carrying them away from the galaxy, across the plane of the disk, in the general direction of the Andromeda Galaxy, M31, in the common plane of the Local Group. Teragon is located at that deep red point about in the middle of the blue disk. They have it marked.

The sense of conversation was an artifact of the way he had grown up, walling off the memories, and of the way he had reconnected them to himself. The effect was weak, but definite. And this "voice," although single, held the incommensurable personalities of both Rael and Nazarine.

A map implies scale of operation. This is a galactic scale map. Whoever used to be here navigated or astrogated on a galactic scale, since this display is the basic picture you get when you activate it. It will doubtless show other things.

Demsing had only turned on what appeared to be the lowest operations level of consoles; he had not turned on those which appeared to be supervisory positions. Now he returned to the dais and the center console, and turned it on, the same way.

At first, there was no apparent change in the presentation, but after a moment, he could see a faint silvery trace, linking the Small Magellanic Cloud with the main galaxy. The trace connected the two in a long ellipse which intersected the galactic disk at the location of the red Teragon Marker, passed "underneath," out the other side of the disk, and back to the Small Cloud.

He stepped back into the seats to look at it. *Yes, that's an orbit, all right. The way it's oriented, that would make the motion of the Teragon System quite different from the motion of the stars around it. The only reason this has not been noticed is probably that Primary is so feeble. Get a parsec away from Primary and you wouldn't even know it was there, unless you were an astrogator, looking for it. And nobody does motion studies of white dwarfs. There are too many of them, and they are too faint. Much more exciting stars to study!*

The "voice" continued, *The stars around these parts are mostly disk stars, orbiting the center of mass in what are basically circular orbits with local motions added-on. An orbit here takes about two hundred million years. That orbit displayed up there would be quite a bit longer, I should guess about three times as long if they stick to straight celestial mechanics without drive systems, which we don't know. Give it a period of eight hundred million years, just to be on the safe side.*

Demsing looked at the display for a long time, trying to understand the implications of that map, in an abandoned and empty auditorium, whose owners were not in evidence. It implied a scale of rational thought which could not adequately be understood. He could not grasp it.

That's just an orbit. It doesn't mean necessarily that they actually flew it as presented. Consider this fact. That when the group of stars we now call our own neighborhood was on the other side of the galaxy, in the same orbit, neither human beings nor the bright marker stars we use for astrogation existed.

Demsing let that information flood into him, and went back to the dais, and turned off the consoles, one by one, returning the display to its inactive state, as he'd found it.

He left the empty auditorium without looking back at it, but his mind was full of the enigma it represented, the questions such an artifact raised. This was something so vast that The Morphodite's ability to manipulate societies and certain causal relationships was rendered of less importance than the heartbeat of an insect.

And he still had to find food, and a way out of here, back to the surface.

14

To anyone who might say that they see light at the end of the tunnel, I answer that there is no light there whatsoever, that there is only and solely the darkness. You do not walk into the heart of darkness which is the deception of contemporary life unless you carry the inextinguishable light with you, within you, well-fueled and protected against the downdrafts of the membraneous wings of unnamed and unnamable things. There is no light at the end of the tunnel: remain in light as long as you can. Remain in light. Remain in light.

H. C., 1984

The hardest thing in life, Demsing thought as he walked through the underground structure, *was realizing what one didn't know.* It was a terror and an unspeakable horror greater than any fear openly acknowledged, and within everyone's deepest secret heart, it was this which aimed and guided the lives of all, even those who claimed bravery. Indeed, those who talked the loudest feared it the most.

The diabolical subtlety of this was most apparent in the lives that all chose to live, finding a structure within which one could seek the narrow excellence. As long as that bubble was never punctured, the assumptions behind it would never be questioned.

He saw it as Demsing-himself, a citizen of Teragon, with its endless transformation into a world of urban gangs—sophisticated and relatively civilized in most cases—and the incredible depth of blindness and ignorance such a habit naturally and easily led them all into. And he also saw it with the continuity of The Morphodite, through all of those-before who he had been, lived those lives. Behind them all loomed another provincial world, Oerlikon, and behind that, still another, and even that one had fallen at the very moment it should have stood and flown, the narrow and ugly dream of narrow and ugly men with their spurious dreams of power and manipulation.

He would have never questioned it, although now he could see the evidence strewn all around the planet, if indeed one could call it that. How had it happened? They had all come there from somewhere else, and they had to come through space. Had they known nothing? Had they covered the viewports up? Were they not curious?

And he saw why Faren had told him nothing, too. That, too. It would have hampered him fatally on Teragon, and above all else she had wanted him to succeed here—that had been her promise to Nazarine. To integrate him completely within the world they had fallen onto, and learn to forget the evil knowledge they had forced somehow onto Rael back in the beginning.

But something about that supposed history seemed to fit into the air of antiquity which invested the corridors and rooms and halls underground. The surface of Teragon had been sealed off from the underground parts, which he now traversed so casually. When they found more tunnels and passages, they wrote them off as someone else's work, and left them in their darkness. Somebody made them. It wasn't important. There was nothing down there. Like that. Teragon was old, too.

So all this had been down there, below, all that time, and how much more time?

Along the main corridor, as he thought of it, he passed other chambers, whose purposes were not immediately apparent. He seemed to be approaching a center of some kind. But there were no signs or symbols on the walls, nor were there any pictures. Whoever these creatures had been, he didn't know much about them, and he thought that they probably would not have appeared human, although the screen on the wall in the auditorium suggested eyes, and a visual band similar to the human norm.

He thought he would have preferred actual ruins, instead of this functioning underground city. Ruins presupposed a lot of things, mostly comfortable to the viewers who came after. But these were not ruins. Nonetheless, Demsing walked along the halls and chambers with more confidence. Maybe the machinery still worked, true, but the uncontacted surface and the emptiness worked together powerfully. There was no one here, and whoever they had been, they had been gone a long time. That itself made their achievements more awesome, and Demsing did not touch many things.

Where were they, when they left Teragon? Had this system been falling empty all the way from the Lesser Magellanic Cloud? Or even longer?

There was one thing which had to be true about this place. It was maintained, and that meant that something maintained it. Somewhere there had to be a device, or a control center, completely automated. He did not have quite enough nerve to call it a computer, although one could do so, with a wide range of meaning for that word.

But he was not looking for it. His main concern was to find something edible, if it existed, and then a way back to the surface. And so far, he had found neither.

As he walked through the underground city, Demsing found rooms of different sizes and configurations, but nothing which he could identify as personal quarters, or anything like a market district. He did find more of the consoles with the ball-switches, those in a complex of chambers that were divided up into cubicles, with a console and a hexagonal screen to each cubicle. In each chamber, there was one console of different arrangement, and that one had a different screen, slightly larger, but the shape suggested that when activated, it would display a screen smaller than that of the more numerous type of console. Again, the air of operational control seemed to be absent, here, in these places, and the only purpose Demsing could imagine for them would be some type of school, or training facility. There were no seats, benches, or anything designed to support a buttocks or any analogous structure. It appeared the creatures stood most of the time.

He kept looking. He had found auditoriums, schools, toilets, and water fountains. If they—whatever their configurations—performed these acts, sooner or later they had to eat, and he felt certain that eventually he would find something.

The main hallway he stayed on had increased in size after the auditorium, and somewhat deeper into the complex, expanded to monumental dimensions, gradually becoming taller then wide, and the width opened up to something approaching a hundred meters. This area seemed to be a center of sorts, a place where many passages entered the main one, and some of them were almost as large. He tried to imagine what this place might have looked like in the heyday of the creatures. Obviously, the width was related to the numbers they could expect, since he had found enough of the small rooms and passages to make a rough guess at their apparent size—something a bit larger than human, but not giant. He also had the impression they were stout, or thick, and were possibly thicker-skinned, perhaps with some kind of heavy hide, probably stiff.

As the walls receded to open up into what could only be a square, he began to see water fountains placed along the walls, more and more of them. The ones he tried all worked. Out in the vast open space, there were also a number of enigmatic structures which looked something like the water fountains, but which were separate from the water facilities. The ceiling soared over head into distances he could not accurately estimate.

The structures seemed to be placed randomly out in the open, and had the paddle-like levers typical of the fountains, but there was no outlet for them. On closer inspection, however, there was a slot below the paddle, which opened into a basin shaped like an abstract design for a seashell. He pressed one.

In strange soundlessness, the slot disgorged a granular meal into the basin. A measured amount. Food? He smelled it, cautiously. The meal had a faint odor, but he couldn't identify it. Some scent, subtly yeasty. It was neither a sweet odor nor pungent. As he smelled it, however, he felt his body respond automatically. His stomach began grumbling, his mouth watered, and he felt an urge to eat the stuff. Hesitating, he tasted it. There wasn't much of a flavor, rather like very bland meal. Demsing reviewed his circumstances, his chances for rescue or escape, and stolidly ate the stuff.

He finished one of the portions off, and sat beside the dispenser to await any effects the stuff might have, understanding that it might have delayed effects hours later when it would be too late. There were no immediate effects, other than a release of the tension he had been feeling, and with no one in sight, Demsing leaned back against the dispenser and drifted off to sleep.

* * *

After a time, he woke up and ate some more, this time two portions. The hall remained the same, the lighting did not vary at all. There was no sense of the passage of Time in this place. Demsing had a chronometer, but it seemed to make little difference. He looked at it, but the figures were meaningless.

Now he had time to look around a little more. He climbed up on top of one of the dispensers and looked as far as he could, down the length of hall to either side. Back where he had come from, he could see the hall narrow and, in the far distance, end. Ahead, in the other direction, the hall narrowed a little, and then continued on, with side-entrances that blurred into meaningless detail farther on. There seemed to be no end to it, that way, and there was no horizon, indicative of curvature. He could not accurately estimate the distance. If it was truly straight, it had to end somewhere up there, because it would eventually intersect the surface if it did not end. But he couldn't make an end out in the smudged details near the perspective vanishing point.

Around the edge of "The Square," as he called it, Demsing found chambers with airlocks which were the receiving-ends of dropshafts from somewhere above. Some of these he entered, and tried to activate, but although the automatic pressure adjustment still operated smoothly, he could not persuade the shafts to operate in reverse, and he suspected that they did not.

Continuing his prowling, he also found the entries of drop-shafts to deeper levels, very similar to the one he had entered, and for the first time, he began to feel hopeful he could find an upshaft. They came down those shafts to this level, which seemed important, and they also had many side-passages running off in every direction, so eventually he thought he'd find one. From what he had seen, the creatures seemed to know where everything was without signs.

He stayed close to the square and made careful observations to make sure he didn't get lost, while he explored, and when he didn't find what he was looking for, went back, ate again, and rested. This was how he came to measure time—by "eats" and "sleeps."

During his explorations, which he continued, Demsing found no evidence of anything resembling a private home, apartments, or barracks—anything which could be construed as a living space, private or public. At the end of an inclined side-passage of quite impressive size, he did find a smaller version of the grand square, but other than smaller size, it seemed not to differ at all from the larger one which he was using as a base.

His image of the creatures who made and used this place made a strange picture in many ways. For instance, since he had an idea of their physical limits, but no idea of the details of their appearance or structure, he substituted a figure in his mind's-eye, and played at imagining the squares and plazas, the tunnels, halls and assembly rooms he had found, filled with the creatures, moving along, gathering, eating, drinking. These imaginary projections were brown in color, stocky and barrel-like, with short limbs, and their outlines were blurred and out of focus, so that one could not see details. And he visualized them as being much more communally minded than humans; they would have liked crowds. And one other thing: they didn't sleep. The absence of private rooms and the unchanging, constant illumination of the underground suggested that.

He was beginning to feel defeated. He had found nothing resembling an upshaft at all, or a lift, and it was beginning to nag at him. They had shafts coming down from higher levels, and they had shafts going lower; they had to have some method of going up, somewhere. In fact, he was near giving up for a time, when he found the top end of an upshaft almost by accident.

He had missed it by an ordinary mistake: Demsing had been looking for airlocks as an indicator of the shafts, and just on a chance, had investigated a small side-passage. This one had ended in a large room quite different from the others he had been in; the creatures seemed to prefer hard, well-defined edges, rather than curving surfaces, and normally their rooms were square or rectangular in plan. This room was quite different. Circular in plan, it was, in its interior space, a torus, formed by a smooth-lipped well in the center, and a downward-pointing projection from the ceiling. The ceiling showed distinct sectioning lines. Here, then, was the upper end of an upshaft, and it worked the same as the others. A blast of air, surging up the shaft, propelled the body to the top, where it would slip over the edge of the lip of the well, onto the floor.

Now that he knew they existed, he redoubled his efforts to find the bottom end of an upshaft.

One more eat and one more sleep, and he found one, at the end of a fairly long passage he risked checking out. Like the downshaft he had come down in, this one was at the end of a long, featureless hall, and was entered through an airlock. There was no difference from the outside to indicate its status or function, but inside, on the inner door, a bas-relief circle had been embossed. Demsing locked the pressure doors and entered the bottom of the upshaft, after the air pressure had equalized.

For a time, nothing happened, and he wondered how they activated it. He tried jumping; nothing happened. So he began a minute examination of the surface of the tube.

It was hard to see, and he might have missed it, but near the pressure door of the airlock, there was one of the ball switches. He rolled it a little, experimentally, and found that it only moved one way. He rolled it to its stop without hesitating.

For a moment, nothing happened, which caused a shock of disappointment and anger to rush through him, but at the moment when he was starting to move, he heard a soft click from somewhere below the grating he was standing on, and the blast of air started. Before it took him, he risked one glance upward, and all he could see was the shaft. Its end was hidden in the soft lighting and the perspective vanishing point somewhere far above.

This was different from falling: in the downshafts, the energy of the falling body had to be braked. Upward, the air blast had both to provide upward motion against gravity, and control the rate. It was not pleasant, and it was very slow starting. After he had found a stabilized position, he was rising very slowly, and he could still see the bottom clearly, when he could clear his eyes in the blast. It was a lot harder than the downshafts, and Demsing did not wonder that the creatures did not have so many of the upshafts. He glanced at his chronometer, and wondered how long it would take to go up the same distance he had fallen down.

After the journey upshaft, Demsing no longer wondered that the creatures of the underworld did not care to go up; it was a long and difficult journey. For the first part, it was slow—not as fast as falling down the downshaft. For another, it went in stages, as if the airlift system somehow wouldn't work so well rising. And that was an experience. When he reached a landing, one of the torus-shaped upshaft receivers, he was dumped over the edge of the well with no ceremony and little braking. Then he had to walk down a short passage to the next stage, enter the upshaft, activate it, and go through the same process all over again, with the certain promise of more bruises at each receptacle. And so it went, through ten stages. Ten more.

By this time, Demsing was both bruised and sore from the landings, and windburned from the air blast coming up the shafts. He picked himself up, and started down the exit passage which would lead to yet another of the upshafts. In all his trips along the passageways, each one had been slightly different. Some were straight, but of various lengths. One in particular had been a long walk. Others went through complicated changes in level and direction before reaching the airlock. So he wasn't surprised when he didn't find an airlock right away. There was only one way out of the well, and Demsing followed it, although wearily.

This one was small and narrow, and the poorest-lit passage yet. Many of the small footlights were broken or inoperative, and the passage turned often, sometimes very sharply, and went up, constantly, but occasionally at a steep enough angle to make him slow down to catch his breath. Still he went on, doggedly, deliberately shutting his mind out and walking on until he found the next airlock sealdoor, which he really didn't want to find.

Afterward, he could not accurately remember how long he walked up that narrow, twisting passageway. Sometimes he dozed off while walking. But at last he did come to an end of the passage. It was partially blocked by rubble, and almost all the lights were out. The ceiling had fallen in.

Behind him was a darkness deeper than dark. Demsing did not know how long he had been walking. Ahead of him the tunnel ended in a loose mound, although at the top, there was clear space, and some weak light beyond. Lethargically, he cleared a hole he could crawl through, stepped over the rest, and found a door. It was different, but he did not care, and so he opened it, and stepped through, into a wide, polished *Kamen* tunnel, with some metal stairs nearby. He looked back at the door. Someone had painted "DANGER—ROCKFALL" across it.

He was back, on the surface of Teragon.

As it turned out, he had twelve more levels to go before he emerged into the weak light of Primary, still wheeling overhead in its eccentric course, but those he didn't mind, nor did he mind finding himself on the far side of The Palterie. He set out for Desimetre immediately, and was halfway there when he realized that he didn't know if he could find the downshaft he had fallen down again. But that was no matter, seen against what he had done, what he had seen. And what he knew. And what he had to do.

15

A most neglected component of the study of perception is the consequence of timing: not so much what we come to know, but when we come to know it. And not only what date, what time, but in resonance and in cadence with what else is being discovered as well as what is already known. The range of expressions of this temporal congruence can reach meaningless entropic noise on the one hand, and on the other, powerful and expressive music which captures the culmination of a moment, an individual, a culture, or a point of history; for good as well as for evil.

H. C., Atropine

Demsing had shed much of his former habit of subtle concealment, and walked openly through Desimetre. It was not so much a move of carelessness or forgetfulness, but a deliberate stance, which would certainly produce results of its own, as well as provide himself with a longer field of view.

Having realized his own layered past, and having come to terms with it, enabled him to assess considerably better than before, when his perceptions had been colored by his own shadow. What he saw as he walked was easy enough to pick out of the general pattern: his appearance had been picked up quickly by wide-flung members of the Wa'an School, and it had been unexpected, but their reaction had been fast, as he would have expected.

As yet, there had been no response, but they remained alert and followed him closely. It was so easy to pick it up. And as for what they might do, he shrugged off. He had read them, down there in the underground, basing his input on things he had known, and deeper things he realized he should have known. It didn't matter much, now, about them: they were powerless and had let control of events pass to others. So they watched him, and he thought: *Let them watch.*

When he neared Klippisch's place, on a street in Desimetre that had become more familiar to him than any other place in the imaginable universe, he noticed that the number of watchers increased, but was divided into two cohorts: one converging on him, obviously with himself as the target, not yet of any action, and another, which had been aimed at something else, but whose aim had now been changed. From what? They had been mobilized as a team to take over Klippisch's operation, apparently, but had stopped to wait for the correct moment, crucial to their pattern of thinking, before proceeding.

As he had almost reached the door to enter the building, a woman who had been just a passing figure suddenly turned her full attention on him, and he knew who she was. Not precisely who, but certainly what. This would be the one who was running this operation. What had she been called? Telny? He turned to the woman and stopped.

Demsing saw by slight betrayals within her motions that she had been told what he could become, and was terrified, under the surface layer of effective and ruthless control. He said, "Yes, I am the one you seek."

It seemed to shake Telny, like a gust of wind, which never blew on Teragon but which they remembered in speech forms whose origins had been lost uncounted years, centuries. She came closer, and asked, "Have you recovered your pasts?"

"Yes. I see Faren has told you. It could have been no one else."

"What do you intend to do?"

Now he hesitated. Could he say it, so baldly? He thought not. Telny was not ready yet. He said, "I need to collect a company of friends, so that we all may address ourselves to something greater than the sum of our disputes. Send your people to other jobs. We have no need for them."

"We?"

"You are certainly invited. But not the entire horde out there. After all, they have been set to locate me, and so here I am. They are no longer required, and you will see that your mission has changed."

"You came as yourself!" It was almost accusatory, as if she expected to see the direct evidence of Change, an adolescent girl.

"Well, of course. Who else would I come as?"

For some reason this seemed to frighten her even more. He added, "Go ahead—do as I ask."

"On faith."

"Oh faith; I have to show you by example what living for the sure thing alone brings us all."

Telny smoothed her hand through her hair, glanced around, and repeated it.

Demsing added, "The Klippisch team, as well."

"We give it all up. Do you know that Dossifey caught Galitzyn, and is bringing him here now?"

He lied, "Yes." Then, "I need Galitzyn, too. He is about to become useful, instead of what he has been, a nuisance."

She made another gesture, and almost immediately Demsing could feel the pressure easing off, the watchers dispersing, the net which had been so carefully assembled, now drifting apart. If he could thread his way through this narrow passage, that dispersal would spread throughout Teragon, propagated by the Wa'an School and all its members.

Telny said, "I am Telny. I lead, here. I will take you at your word, although I see no evidence of the powers of which I was told."

"The problem with this most difficult art that I was taught, and devised in part in an earlier version of myself, is that it cannot be demonstrated convincingly: it can only be used. I do not wish to waste valuable people."

"Surely you could find a target that doesn't matter so much."

Demsing shook his head. "They are all valuable. Priceless, in fact."

"Then you will extract your price for Chalmour?" She had read his answer completely wrong. How could this woman be so effective and still be so dense to what he was trying to tell her?

He said, slowly, "How should I punish you for permitting the one act which put you and your organization within my reach? You are here, and you speak before acting: do you need any more proof? And if there is to be talk of revenges, then let's speak instead of that girl you wrote off and sent against me in Meroe. There was a crime you should feel proper guilt over."

She protested, "That was an internal matter, a routine sanction against insoluble flawing! You have no right to question that, especially since your actions dispatched her!"

"I released her, that is true. That is why I have the right. And that is what I am going to change."

"Then we will have no more control. If we don't have death as a bottom line, we can no longer enforce our disciplines."

"When you have to use force, you're wrong from the start, no matter what you say." He turned into the building. "Come inside. We have others to meet."

Telny, disoriented by the unexpected responses, followed him, saying, "There is no one here except Chalmour and a scrub team of apprentices under Weenix and Slezer, unwashed recruits from Petroniu and the more disreputable parts of The Palterie."

Demsing entered the office, saying over his shoulder, as if Telny no longer mattered, "They seem to be doing well enough." And he saw Chalmour, behind Klippisch's desk, looking in his direction, but not precisely at him, as if she wanted to see him, and yet wanted not to see him. The apprentices let him pass unchallenged, and he covered the distance, and those few meters seemed to take forever, while she continued to stare at the door, only daring to watch him with her peripheral vision, as he approached the chair, and touched her gently across the back, just below her neck, and he could feel the tension in her, the muscles held rigid, the artificial light of the office making her pale skin even paler. She turned her face toward Demsing slowly, not yet daring to speak, nor would anyone else. Chalmour stood up, turning and suddenly reached for him and grasped him tightly. Demsing enfolded her within the circle of his arms, holding her as tightly as she held him.

Telny said, after a time, "Of course, we regret any events which may have taken place while. . . ."

Both of them turned to stare at Telny after her snide reminder. She fell silent, as much from what she saw in Chalmour's eyes as for what she saw in Demsing's. But it was Demsing who spoke for them. "That has no power over me, and you have none over her. Remember that."

"We will see what power we have."

Demsing sighed. "This is tiresome. You will cease such word-bandying or I will write you out of the Teragon that is to be. Understood?" Telny fell silent. He said, "You allowed me to reach Chalmour. That was your mistake. As long as you could reach her before me I could not act on your organization

with my skill. But it's too late, now. I can do what
I need to, and protect Chalmour, who ties me to
you. Test me once more and you yourself will live
to see the example you asked for."

Telny could not mistake what he said, or the
conviction in his voice. Finally, she said, "Very
well. But I will say one more thing. It is my understanding that you have to concentrate on your
inner vision in order to see it."

Demsing nodded. "That was true at one time.
With each successive version, the routine of sepa-
ration of perceptions has become less necessary. I
can call it up now, just by wanting it. I can see the
possibilities even as we talk, and there are many
ways to enter that. Many, not just one. Of course,
each one has its trade-offs, this, here; that, there:
slight change according to the way I approach it.
While I have spoken to you in this sentence I have
seen fourteen distinct ways to write you and your
organization off. It is only because I need you, we
all need you, that I refrain from doing so."

Telny, clearly, was not accustomed to this kind
of talk, and totally without proof, too. But when it
came to testing it with action, something held her
back, if for no better reason than to hear what he
had to say. She stepped back, conscientiously relaxed; she had performed more interrogations than
she could remember in her life, and all the signs of
deep truth were on Demsing; it didn't matter if he
could do what he said or not, in the abstract: he
believed he could do it. More than that: he *knew*
he could do it. In many, far too many cases, will
and belief were sufficient.

There was a commotion by the door, a spattering of angry words, and Klippisch, Dossifey, and Galitzyn entered the room. Klippisch was still remonstrating with Galitzyn, who was unable or unwilling to argue with her. Dossifey had him tied by the thumbs, behind, and was absentmindedly leading him around like an unwilling specimen of livestock, grinning like an idiot.

When Klippisch saw who was present, she stopped short, breathed deeply, and began again. "Demsing! Where in the hell have you been? We have been ransacking the planet looking for you, and here you are, and you have brought one of those nightcrawlers with you!" She referred to Telny at the last.

He answered, "I see Dossifey has located our missing Galitzyn, who might also answer to the name of Pitalny Vollbrecht."

"That, and more he'll answer to," Klippisch exclaimed. "Bad enough he runs off, but now I can't find a replacement anywhere, and the house surrounded with the night-demons." She leered at Galitzyn suggestively, with a glance which promised good. "Slezer has been slack in his interrogations! Some practice he shall have!" She paused for breath, and added, for effect, "We'll use the Mad Dentist Procedure Number Five! Slezer! Bring the leg irons!"

Galitzyn, it was true, had lost considerable color and in fact looked slightly greenish, a pale gunmetal sheen on his skin.

Demsing said again, "I don't think we need Slezer and his hands of thumbs. I think Ser Vollbrecht might be willing to discuss things with us in plain language."

Galitzyn nodded, hopefully, although his smile faded when he looked at Klippisch, who still seemed to want torture, if only in principle.

Telny said, softly, "Klippisch, do you remember that remarkable tale that was circulating, say, about thirty-five standard years ago, about a changeling?"

Klippisch stopped, looked about absently for a moment, and answered, "Yes, I do, now that you mention it. Loose on one of the big ships. But never any more than that."

"Demsing is that changeling."

Galitzyn-Vollbrecht rolled his eyes, and groaned. Demsing said, "Yes, it is true. And for you, Galitzyn, you know what I am. You came all this way to do something with me. And so you know that I have remembered. I remember it all. So ask me openly— what do you want with me?"

Galitzyn looked from face to face, and saw no relief there, not from any of them. Now that it was all out, he had no friends on this feral planet. He said, "It began when Kham failed to return. We were also notified of Palude's suicide. But there was no report, nothing. And no idea of the where-abouts of The Morphodite. On Heliarcos we knew that we had lost track of it in space, and it was only a matter of time until it would appear there. So the Regents . . . closed the whole complex down, and left. To the four winds. The entire facility! Pompitus Hall! The Black Projects were only part— the smallest part, but they closed it all down!"

Demsing asked, casually, "So where are they now?"

"No one knows. They destroyed all the records, closed down all funding, covert links, and ran. They were doing other projects, apparently things like the Morphodite, that they didn't want known in general circulation. They left them high and dry. There is all kinds of trouble out there, on these isolated planets."

He paused for breath, and then continued, "We had to work on the quiet, you understand. All of us who were left behind had to find other positions on Heliarcos, and not all made it. Some became miners, or janitors. It was a hard time."

Demsing said, "Jedily Tulilly sympathizes with your suffering."

Galitzyn said, "We traced you here, to Teragon. We wanted to set things right, and we wanted to ask your help. It was then that we found out that you didn't know anything of your past, and then we didn't know what would happen, if you found out by accident. It seemed worse, in the light of what you seemed to have become. I was sent here to find a way."

Demsing said, "The operations you spoke of: their failure was what Nazarine went through Change to make happen. It has gone too far now to change that."

"We didn't want them salvaged. No. We just wanted you to help us rebuild them. The Regents left us with the bills, and the responsibilities. Their problems are beyond what we can solve."

"We wanted to make sure that sort of thing

would be difficult to set up again. The tales of the horror stories will circulate forever. Mankind has another in its pantheon of villains." Demsing finished, sadly. "Those Regents, they should have read more fiction before they started. An ancient tale, 'Frankenstein,' says it all."

"Would you have helped us?"

"Probably not. But I would have answered you directly. You see, when you do one of these operations that I do, you pay a kind of price for it: once set in motion, the consequences can't be redone. The act of alteration makes that sequence immune to further alteration. Rael knew this. I know it a lot better. The continued use of the powers of The Morphodite tends to build a rigid universe with no flex in it. It needs flex. Without that, it breaks. The breaks appear in the macrocosm as destructive natural phenomena. It's like the reverse of magic, in that use of the power builds a universe immune to any power. It becomes locked in. I cannot save you from your own evil. Only you can do that."

"I see. Then you have no further use of me?"

Klippisch barked, "Not so fast. I have business with the good academician Pitalny Vollbrecht about an unexpired contract!"

Telny said, "Your requirements for us are obviously gone. So we would like to be paid."

Demsing said, "There is nothing I can do for you; but there is something you can do for me."

Galitzyn stopped short, struck at Demsing's obvious sincerity. "What do you have in mind?"

Demsing asked, "You have a faculty, back on Heliarcos?"

"Dispersed somewhat, and in deep trouble, but yes."

"All kinds of experts, specialists, scientists?"

"Yes, all sorts. Xenobiologists, Cyberneticists, Natural Scientists, Theorists, Philosophers. . . . Why?"

"We have a grand mystery for them to solve, here, and to assist us to find a way off Teragon. This planet is not a natural object."

Galitzyn looked alertly at Demsing. So did the rest of them. He asked, "What is it, then?"

"It's a spaceship. Totally artificial, inside and out. And older than anything we've run across before. And its owners have vanished without a trace."

16

We are vehicles for things which speak through us, and we can sometimes relate these things to totemic spirits whose symbols are drawn from exemplars in the animal world: Raven, Eagle, Coyote, Wolf. These are some of the more obvious symbols—but there are others, equally powerful, who have no symbolic form borrowed from nature.

H. C., Atropine

Thelledy had taken charge of the team assigned to capture Galitzyn, and she had reported their discovery, expecting to get back, from Telny, the signal to proceed. Instead, what she got back was an order to cease and desist, and to disengage immediately. For a moment, she considered going on without orders. She believed that with a little extra effort, she could run the offworlder to earth. But in the end, she backed off and instructed her people to disperse. It was true that if she disregarded the order and succeeded quickly, there would be no strenuous objection, at the least no punishment. But if she had miscalculated, and

Galitzyn remained missing, while she continued, then the risk started to increase.

When she had seen to it that all her team members were out of the area, she left, herself, walking quite openly through the streets, going nowhere in particular.

This had all been easy for a long time, almost a routine operation, with no contact. Everything had worked within the bounds of the expected. But since the Meroe incident, things had been drifting astray, none of them going right. Yes, Meroe. That's where they could trace it from, although the apparent diversion from plan hadn't actually begun until long after Demsing had returned to Desimetre.

She shook her head. They still didn't know who had actually killed Asztali, even though Demsing was the most likely suspect. But why kill her at all? Certainly not for revenge—he already had that, from the Carrionflower. But it was after that, that he had started looking for Vollbrecht, so he got that from Asztali, but how had she known that? There was a slip, somewhere. She had heard or found something she had not been allowed to have, and so ... they had set her up, knowing that he tended to do things like that when pressed, hard. She would have carried an antidote, obviously, but if the contents had been switched, the injection would have had no effect, and there she would have been. The conclusion was inescapable.

They wanted him to move out of the Meroe area, but no one reasonably expected him to return to Desimetre, and walk almost into the middle of the contact point. And with him asking about Vollbrecht they couldn't risk moving him again. He saw too far.

She had faith in the organization of which she was a part. That was not the question. But there was no denying that things had not worked right since then.

And she was being followed, herself. She had just picked that up, and had not been aware of it. She looked about, but saw nothing out of order. A street somewhere in Desimetre, descending down the slope slantwise, curving, following an imaginary contour. This part of Desimetre was more given to residences, and most of them occupied little courtyards, behind low garden walls. Not a good place for tracking, so whoever it was seemed to have a good grasp on the fundamentals. And who might it be?

They had lost track of Demsing, so he was a possibility. More than just possible, and the thought of that made the skin on the back of her neck prickle.

Thelledy made an effort to maintain her original pace, without revealing her suspicions. But now, she changed the general direction, at an intersection where the street forked, the main channel going off downhill more steeply, and the other, to the left, starting back up the rise. She had some of her own methods of clarifying situations like these.

For a long time, she strolled on, seemingly aimlessly, but there was direction in her way. Near the top of the rise, there was a certain restaurant which had several ways in and out of it, and she knew that she could either lose her shadow there, or confirm who it was. Whoever it was would have to come in close, or lose her, and she thought they might see that. But the sensation continued without a ripple.

When she reached the restaurant, she went directly into the cavernous interior, which was broken up into several areas, then up the stairs to the second level, where she faded into the dim background and waited.

She didn't have long to wait. She saw someone come in, just as she had, giving the whole show away by looking around. She sighed. An amateur, at the crucial moment. It was Ilyen. She glanced around the restaurant, and saw that others had seen what he was doing. She made a hand sign, which he caught out of the corner of his eye, looked again, and found her. He smiled sheepishly, and came up the stairs to join her.

She motioned for him to sit, and he did. She said, "Not so good, your grand entrance! Even the proles picked you out."

"Well, by then it didn't matter. It looked like you were headed here, so I thought it would be a good place to catch up with you."

"Such as it is, you have found me."

"Have you given any thought to the general situation we might be in?"

"Relative to what?"

"Specifically, to the fact that we have no idea where Demsing might be, or what he's doing." There was a curious eagerness about him.

She said, "Go on."

"I know where he is."

"He, or someone like him?"

"Demsing. He's at Klippisch's place. I saw him there. Walked in right in the open. Telny was there, and when she gave the signal to disperse, I stayed. He's there all right, and they found Galitzyn, too, so all of them are in one place."

"And you came looking for me."

"Yes. They are all there, talking."

Thelledy studied Ilyen for a long time. Finally, "You are perhaps trying to tell me something?"

He sat back in the narrow chair, and shrugged. "There is an opportunity, there, to accomplish many ends."

"Where is Telny?"

"Inside, with them. Demsing invited her, and she went."

Thelledy turned away. "It's no business of mine, now. Or yours. I can't go back there."

"It wouldn't take long."

"To do what?"

"Settle things with Demsing. This has been going all against us, and that comes from him. We could settle this for all time."

"You're out of your mind. We'd never get in, much less do anything."

"There are no guards; the ways are open."

"What about Telny?"

"Include her with them. It's done, then we negotiate."

"With whom? And for what?"

"Galitzyn and Klippisch." He didn't say for what.

"Why break with the organization?"

Here Ilyen paused, as if collecting his thoughts

238 • M.A. Foster

carefully. He began, "See, the loyalty you mention
only works one way. When it comes to it going
downhill, then it's excuses. Consider Asztali. . . ."

Thelledy considered, and remembered that Ilyen
had been, to use a euphemism, "quite close" with
Asztali. "Go on. But I know about that: they had
her up for punishment . . ."

"Shuck and jive. You heard it from them. I heard
it different. There was no offense, there was no
punishment. She was considered expendable, something to buy Demsing to move. All the antidotes in
her kit were dummied. How do you like that? You
might be next, and over something even more
trivial."

"How do you know this?"

"I have it from the ordinance-keeper. Orders from
on high, she said, dummy the drug kit. No reason,
nothing. But it was obvious they wanted Asztali to
fail. She wasn't failing anything, as you have doubtless been told. She was one of the best, and more
than a little troublesome to some of the old farts
who were catching a free ride. The plan was, he'd
trap her, and see who it was, and that would flush
him out. Mind, he was hard to follow in Meroe.
But nobody imagined he was going to hear 'Vollbrecht' from her. Nobody ever overrode a Carrionflower before. So he moved more than they wanted."

"So that was why you worked Chalmour over? I
kept quiet when you told Telny I gave the order.
Yes, I see that."

"I almost blew it, but yes, there's an element of
that. But the main thing is that you know, out of
this, that you can't trust them anymore. All up

and down the line: you provide them with the foundation to act in the first place, and they sell you out cheap whenever they feel like it. Asztali is not the only one."

"Why act now, specifically?"

"Demsing. Telny is going to cut a private deal with Demsing. He's been on to something from the start, and now it's all going to come out. The world is going to change. And the Organization? Poof, poof, piffles: The old ladies get retirement and the operators get retraining. That is, we will graciously be allowed to step and fetchit."

Thelledy listened with shock and disbelief, but there was a certain ring to Ilyen's accusations which she could not deny. It was, she thought, a bad place to be in, because none of the choices looked especially good. If Ilyen was right, and he had assembled a powerful argument, then all the time, the work, the things they had done without, all that would be for nothing, when the new deal was cut. Demsing, Galitzyn, Telny, all in on the new world, and the rest of us cut out of it. And if he was wrong? That line of thought was simply unspeakable. If they were quick, they could probably sell out to Klippisch, but that would only be temporary. The problem with treason is that if you spend it for trifles, then it's gone forever. You had no value to anyone. And it was treason, no doubt about it. The question was, what could they buy with it?

"Why me?"

He did not hesitate. "After it's done, one negotiates, the other signals . . . supporters in other places.

And as for why you, it's that we've had you in sight for a long time. We were fairly certain you'd see the worth of our argument, without bolting and blowing the whistle, and so far, you've listened. Haven't you?"

"Yes, but I. . . ."

"So go ahead and report it. Then what if I'm right? Then you threw away your only chance, for nothing. Or bow out of it, say nothing, and then I'll do nothing, and what-if?"

Thelledy felt herself under enormous pressure to choose a course and act on it, but there was something murky, concealed about this, too. She thought, not entirely clearly, but accurately enough, that if she was being brought into it this late, it was obvious that she wouldn't rate very highly in the new order, either, and that thought had an air of wistful sadness to it. Things never became easier as one grew older. That was what we all missed about childhood. Things were clear, then.

As if divining her thought, Ilyen added, "I know. There aren't any good choices anymore. Still one must bet on something. You can't just pass, because that's a choice, too."

And she thought, that she should negotiate some kind of agreement with Ilyen, as for her place, afterward, but that was a pointless idea. Ilyen was already a traitor. If he broke one loyalty, others would mean even less. And she thought she saw something else, too: that such a plan could only have layers of backup contingency plans behind it. If Ilyen walked out of here alone, she would never leave alive. She risked a glance around the room, at the people she had identified as a random collection of Proles, and saw, at a deeper look, that that was exactly what she had been supposed to see. The room was flickering and alive with an active net.

In the end, it was not fear that decided her, but the simple existence of the network, controlled by Ilyen. If they had gone that far, and were operating clandestinely already at that level, then this had deep roots, indeed, and it might be better to go with it. And as a final aside to her own sense of guilt, she added that she had never cared that much for Demsing, anyway.

"What sort of plan do you have in mind?"

"Knives, front and rear. You to do the back door. I take the front, and wait for you to move. One-two, crossfire. It will have to be fast."

"Fast I can handle. How do I know you'll come in?"

"Because you know one can't do it, and you know I wouldn't ask if I thought I could do it alone. And as far as trapping you, well, there are easier ways of doing that, at a much lower level of loss. Point?"

"Point."

"We finish that, then holdfast. They'll talk."

"You're sure about that?"

"There will be backup from my side. In on signal."

"Now?"

"Yes," he said, getting to his feet. "But one thing more. I want Chalmour for my own purposes, unharmed."

Thelledy shrugged, standing up. "Why not?" Although she did so with a certain fatalism. Already Ilyen's regime looked less attractive than the one he would replace. Perhaps there was a way, too, to line all of them out; yes. There was a way. Once he came in on her entry, there would be no turning back. Tricky, but it would work. A double-cross, and then a quick alibi. She might escape this yet.

17

You never know when you are going to have to make your stand. It might be right here, right now. Might not be. Might be never, you never know.

H. C., Atropine

Everyone except Galitzyn was surprised at Demsing's announcement. Galitzyn nodded and said, "Teragon has been regarded as suspicious for a long time. Surveys picked up all kinds of things that don't add up, but the trouble is, no one has ever had time to run it down. There is simply too much to do, too many objects to study. But I'll tell you what I know about Teragon and Primary. For one thing, White Dwarfs don't have oxygen-atmosphere planets. To get to be white dwarfs, they blow out any planetary systems they might have had. The few which are known possess a few lumps of slag, and the rocky remnants of gas giant cores. Also the orbit of Teragon is odd in two ways, no, three: it doesn't orbit in the plane of Primary's equator, it's in far too close to have the physical features it does, and its orbit is too close to a circle—the eccentricity is so small it can't be measured from outside the system."

He stopped to catch his breath, and then went on, "Primary is odd, too. Primary, judging by its percentages of heavy metals, is an extremely old star, and it has an anomalous galactic orbit. Surveys mark it off as one of the halo stars with an eccentric orbit, tilted so that it intersects the galactic disk. It just happens to be passing through the disk in this era, otherwise no one would ever have seen it. Nobody is studying individual halo stars, and besides, you can't even see a white dwarf much farther off than ten parsecs. I know it's odd. Why do you think Teragon is a ship?"

"Because I found an area, deep under, where the owners used to live. I saw their instruments."

"You weren't hallucinating?"

"There was food and water. I was down there a long time. I could not have lived without those things. There was a large space, like an auditorium, with display consoles, which I turned on. It showed the galaxy, and the outer satellite systems. The orbit for Primary has its far end out at the Lesser Magellanic Cloud."

"But you saw no one down there?"

"No one, no trace, no nothing. They have been gone a long time. Everything works, but the builders are gone. They left no pictures, nothing. I only saw part of it; there seems to be no end to it, and I never saw anything like a control room. It will take years to unravel everything that is down there.

But some of the displays show writing, so eventually, someone should be able to wear it down."

"How far down?"

"I'm guessing, but the upper part I explored started maybe seventy-five kilometers down, maybe more. You get there by falling down an air shaft which blows a countercurrent against you. Apparently they thought that was a fine way to travel. I didn't much care for it, but it works."

Demsing turned to Telny. "Do you see, now, why I asked you here? This is an unknown which makes all our wars pointless. We could become one people."

Telny said, "Yes. True, but we could also become a planet of impoverished souvenir-peddlers to the great and mighty folk who'd stop by on the grand tour, all those offworld swells."

"We could learn to use it, instead of riding passively on it. We would be the cutting edge. We already have the basic talent here; we combine and refine. I think, somewhere down in that underground, there is a control room, from which we can fly this world anywhere we want. We could have a real sun, and an outside, instead of this nighted city."

Telny nodded. "I see that well enough. So what do we need them for, Galitzyn-Vollbrecht and his offworlders?"

Demsing answered, "We are street-wise, but we have forgotten much of the whole range of our ancestors. No one here has the background now to comprehend everything down there. We're the most sophisticated, most urbanized people in the human universe, and we're primitives. If we take that underworld without understanding what we have, it will be like handing a piece of fine art to a Barbary ape: we will destroy the record preserved down there, and then each other. The point is to integrate ourselves, and then ourselves with the rest who are out there. Pull together instead of flying apart, each of us alone in our specialist culture. We start that here, on Teragon."

"You argue for peace, not war, but I know you know the value of war, and survival."

"I do. But peace is the way, here. We can have it all, but we have to learn to combine, work together. The universe has become a place with too many unknowns. I did not understand that before, but I do now. It always was that way, but we went our own ways far too long."

Demsing said, to Galitzyn-Vollbrecht, "And this is the place where Pompitus Hall can redeem its reputation, and regain, by your own efforts, not mine, your place." He noticed that Dossifey had not untied his thumbs, yet, and asked him to. Presently, Galitzyn was rubbing his wrists and massaging his thumbs. And considering possible outcomes.

Then he asked Klippisch if he could invite Faren in on the discussion they were having, that it was important that she be here as well.

Klippisch agreed, "Yes. I can see a kind of logic behind what you are saying, but I'd like to hear her speak, too. She's an offworlder as well, but she adapted here. It would be quicker if Dossifey called her." She gestured with her head, and Dossifey faded out of the room, still smiling, to find a communicator out of the office.

Once, when Demsing had let The Morphodite flood into him, and seen how to change causality, he had glimpsed the possibilities of a certain design. Now he saw, with that part of his mind which perceived such things, that this design moved from a possibility to something *between*, a potential. He felt its energy, its *rightness*, its justice, but he also felt the price of activating it. There was a sadness to that. He could see it clearly, but there was no other way. A weight was settling on this room, this time, slow ponderous, planetary in mass, more than planetary, balancing, shifting, moving. He could feel the weight. Yes. He had moved Dossifey out of the room. When he came back, he would be out of position. He looked about him: *they* felt nothing, they sensed nothing. It needed one more step ... now ....

Demsing motioned to Klippisch that she should assume her rightful seat behind her own desk and preside over the discussions. And she did it, stepping around Demsing and Chalmour, who were still holding each other tightly. Yes. One more block fitted into place. The mass around him he could feel settled more securely. This had happened to Phaedrus, but accidentally. He hadn't had enough knowledge and skill to move it. And just as accidentally, the focus had moved on, later, settling on someone else. That was the way of it. The people who were upholders of their world never knew it, or if they did, they always tried to manipulate it after it had passed on to another upholder. Even now, he wasn't in complete control of it. It settled on him and upon Chalmour, together. Klippisch sat in her chair and pulled it up close to the desk. Yes. Even better.

All this time, Galatzyn and Telny had been talking, in low tones, exploring the possibilities.

Galitzyn caught his attention. "Yes. You say there was no trace of the creatures down there, none whatsoever?"

"None. There wasn't even a scent of them. The place was clean, the air was recycled, everything worked, the fountains still ran water, and the dispensers still made food-stuff. I had no trouble with any of it. But it felt like they had been gone for a long time. I saw no trace of violence or disease; perhaps whatever maintains the underground could have cleaned that up as well, but surely something would have been broken. We're guessing. We don't know, at least until we can get a crew down there working in that auditorium. I had the feeling about that place, that if you could control those consoles, you could eventually bring it all up. The answers are there, just more than one alone could operate. We have to work together."

Galitzyn agreed. "Absolutely. We have some people who can winkle it out. It'll take time to get them here, though. Did you sense any need for haste?"

"None down there. They are gone, so it would seem. But I feel some haste up here, in this world."

Telny said, "I know. I can feel the pressure of it. But I also see that you are right in this. It has to be all of us, doesn't it?"

"If we continue fighting over scraps, the unknown things slink out of the hidden parts of the forest and bite us while we engage each other."

"Well-said, indeed! Often I have said that very thing to my own trainees, but it is hard to get them to see that. *I* forget it sometimes."

Demsing still maintained contact with Chalmour, but he reached forward, and moved a large glass paperweight over a few centimeters toward Klippisch.

Telny, alert to minutiae as ever, saw the action, but saw no reason for it, and that was what set her internal alarms off. An action without a reason was a clear break in the pattern. And what was it Faren had said? Yes: . . . *it would leave a water tap running, or move a trash can over a meter to the left,* and *you would never see the hand that smote you. It would all come unraveled, and you would never see it.* What was Demsing doing? Was the talk deception, for him to make his random moves in this room, to bring another world-sequence into being? But there was no lie in his voice: he believed deeply in what he had said, here. *I'm seeing him set something up, seeing it happen in front of me, and who knows what reaction he's preparing for?* She thought of moving the paperweight back, but hesitated. *Suppose that's the move I'm supposed to make? Then what?*

But for now he seemed to be satisfied by that move and made no more, and her attention was recalled to Klippisch and Galitzyn, who were still arguing possibilities, and how to bring still others into it. She felt her own control over this world slipping as she stood here, but Demsing seemed satisfied, withdrawn, content. He had brought forth his message, and now was moving into the sidelines, and she didn't understand that, either.

And from Demsing's point of view, each action now caught the onrushing future into a tightening vise, but it wasn't tight enough yet; like the zen archers of old, he was waiting for the perfect moment of precise tension in the string, the bow, and the sublime emotion of allowing the target to aim him, and the last act which would propel the arrow into Time. Yes, now that he took the burden from its nameless predecessor, he felt its power, its inertia, its mass, and its price: as it settled onto him, he felt his visions of himself fading away, an egoless awareness which was the only prelude to action.

They continued to talk, but it was unimportant now, and he only listened, agreeing sometimes, more often saying nothing. He had had to give up this world and its deeds to transform it. The secrets of the underground were no longer his. Yes, this was the right way.

After a time, Faren appeared at the door, and came in. She expressed no surprise at seeing Demsing, instead of what he might have been, the nameless girl who would have been roughly contemporary with Chalmour. Demsing left Chalmour where she was, by the corner of the desk, and as she turned to follow him with her stance, she stepped in front of Klippisch's only route from behind the desk, should threat come through the door.

Demsing briefly hugged Faren, and as she came farther into the room, he turned with her so that Faren was between Telny and himself. Dossifey came back, from the other door, but turned to the window behind Klippisch. It was moving into position like something in slow motion, under water, an effortless glide. Then he felt fear, but he shrugged it off. It would be just like Change, wouldn't it? Maybe easier than Change.

He was looking toward Dossifey's door, and he saw it burst open, and behind it, Thelledy with a short, slightly curved blade, held before her like a spear. She was diversion, and Dossifey and Telny moved instantly to break her flight. He did not look back, but he felt the shadow behind him, the ice-bite of the knife, and that would be Ilyen. Too late, Telny realized her mistake and was turning, but Faren was in her way; there was no way she could clear the older woman in time. Klippisch reached for the paperweight, missed it, and lunged for the side, but Chalmour blocked her, too. Dossifey tripped Thelledy, and drew his knife as she fell.

Demsing fell forward, curling as he settled to the floor, to miss Thelledy, and he watched impassively as Chalmour took Klippisch's knife—Klippisch let her have it—and as Ilyen smiled knowingly at her, she deftly grasped his hair with her right hand, and jerked, and as his head came up, cut his throat. Demsing felt Thelledy bump up against him, grow rigid, and then relax.

He felt the weight lift off him, in just the way he had known it would. It had worked.

Faren and Chalmour bent down to him, both of

them with eyes wild. It was dim now in the office, dimmer than even the poor daylight of Primary. Only seconds. He saw Telny's face, too, upside down. He said, "This was the only way I could do it. Faren knows what Nazarine told her."

Faren said, "You are Nazarine?"

"Yes, Nazarine, Phaedrus, all of them, Damisto-fiya, Rael, Jedily. Yes. All, and Demsing, too. They knew, a long time ago, ancient history, human sacrifice, only they couldn't find the right one, and they turned away from the way to find the one. I saw that I could make it all right, here, now, but the price was myself. And at least one more."

He heard Dossifey. "Thelledy's dead. Ilyen soon will be."

Chalmour cried at him, "Why? Why?"

"Had to be. Got worse if it went any other way. Horrors, reduced to rats in the ruins. Now you have a future, Chal'; use it and don't look back. It will work. Telny!"

The upside-down figure spoke, "Here!"

"Take care of Chalmour: she's your life, now. Faren knows. Ask her. Chalmour has the foundation . . ." Demsing thought that it had gotten very dark, and that he was still talking, there wasn't enough time to say what he had to, and besides, he didn't think they could hear him. No, this was much easier than Change. He smiled, and wondered what he would look like when he woke up.

There were five left standing in the office, and they all stood, and reached across Demsing to touch hands. Klippisch, Telny, Faren, Galitzyn, Chalmour, in silence. It was Telny who broke the silence, at last, amid the fearsome scents of violent death and fear still in the air of the room.

"We know what we have to do."

"Let us begin," said Klippisch.

Chalmour bent down and touched Demsing, but did not cry.

Faren said, "He wanted to use his curse and his gift for us, once, instead of against us, to even the balance of all that had gone before. I do not understand the workings of this, but I know how Nazarine saw what could be, and what the price was for actualizing the things that could become. And so here, Demsing, the same, saw what good there was in us, and how to preserve it and strengthen it, before we were swamped by the unknown that has always been all around us, whether we saw it or not. We cannot see it, but we will act it out, according to what was set in motion, here."

Telny stepped forward. "I understand some of these things in a small part, from what I have known. Let us use this well; such as these are unique. As we all are, unknowing."

DAW

DAW Books now in select format

Hardcover:

☐ **ANGEL WITH THE SWORD**
by C.J. Cherryh
0-8099-0001-7 $15.50/$20.50 in Canada

A swashbuckling adventure tale filled with breathtaking action, romance, and mystery, by the winner of two Hugo awards.

☐ **TAILCHASER'S SONG**
by Tad Williams
0-8099-0002-5 $15.50/$20.50 in Canada

A charming feline epic, this is a magical picaresque story sure to appeal to devotees of quality fantasy.

Trade Paperback

☐ **THE SILVER METAL LOVER**
by Tanith Lee
0-8099-5000-6 $6.95/$9.25 in Canada

THE SILVER METAL LOVER is a captivating science fiction story—a uniquely poignant rite of passage. "This is quite simply the best sci-fi romance I've read in ages."—*New York Daily News*.

NEW AMERICAN LIBRARY
P.O. Box 999, Bergenfield, New Jersey 07621

Please send me the DAW BOOKS I have checked above. I am enclosing $_____ (check or money order—no currency or C.O.D.'s). Please include the list price plus $1.50 per order to cover handling costs.

Name _____

Addres _____

City _____ State _____ Zip Code _____

Please allow at least 4 weeks for delivery

DAW

DAW BRINGS YOU THESE BESTSELLERS BY
MARION ZIMMER BRADLEY